The Beauty of Ordinary Things

"This beautiful short novel is populated by characters who are connected to each other by filaments of memory, regret and yearning. Each strand is lovely on its own, and the whole is captivating, radiant, mysterious, and deeply moving. I loved it."
—ANN PACKER, author of *The Dive from Clausen's Pier* and
Swim Back to Me

"A gorgeous meditation on love and spirit, grief and passion, that unfolds with startling elegance. It captivated and moved me in equal measure."
—CAROLINA DE ROBERTIS, author of *Perla*

Lydia Cassatt Reading the Morning Paper

A #1 Indie Next Pick

"A lovely, moving book — elegant in its economy, delicately powerful."
—TRACY CHEVALIER, author of *Girl with a Pearl Earring*

"Harriet Scott Chessman's prose moves with the deceptive beauty of a ballet dancer, its weightless grace diverting attention from the muscularity powering every gesture."
—Karen Jenkins Holt, *Bookreporter*

"Written in the precise, yet elliptical style of Virginia Woolf."
—*The New York Times*

"Chessman, like Lydia [Cassatt], has allowed herself to inhabit another's world with grace and humility."
—*San Francisco Chronicle*

"Entrancing...heartbreaking...Makes [itself] felt long after one has finished the book."   —*New York Newsday*

"Elegantly conceived and tenderly written."
—*Publishers Weekly*

"A moving story of courage and creativity. ... Pitch-perfect prose ... a celebration of family, love, and art."
—*Arizona Daily Star*

Someone Not Really Her Mother

A GOOD MORNING AMERICA Book Club selection
A *San Francisco Chronicle* "Best Book of 2004"
A Readers Club of America Selection
An Indie Next Reading Group Pick

"Deft, impressionistic prose...[a] haunting novel of memory and its loss."
—SUSAN VREELAND, author of *The Girl in Hyacinth Blue* and *The Boating Party*

"Chessman paints word pictures bathed in color and light."   —*Boston Globe*

Harriet Scott Chessman

THE BEAUTY *of* ORDINARY THINGS

Harriet Scott Chessman has taught literature and writing at Yale University, Bread Loaf School of English, and Stanford University's Continuing Studies Program. She is the author of three acclaimed novels as well as *The Public Is Invited to Dance*, a book about Gertrude Stein. Her fiction has been translated into ten languages. She lives in the San Francisco Bay Area.

HarrietChessman.com

ALSO BY HARRIET SCOTT CHESSMAN

The Public Is Invited to Dance
Ohio Angels
Lydia Cassatt Reading the Morning Paper
Someone Not Really Her Mother

THE BEAUTY *of* ORDINARY THINGS

To Marissa, Micah, and Gabriel

And in memoriam

Mother Placid Dempsey, O.S.B.

and

Mother Irene Boothroyd, O.S.B.

THE BEAUTY *of* ORDINARY THINGS

You choose the rose, love, and I'll make the vow
And I'll be your true love forever.

("Red is the Rose," Irish song)

Succisa virescit.

One

1. Sister Clare

May 13th, 1974

1:20 a.m., before Matins

*I was in a house — in Italy I think — with high, broken
ceilings and blasted walls. Outside, bombs were falling. There
was a war. Terrified, rushing from room to room, I discovered
a staircase filled with rubble. I climbed up and pushed open a
door onto a large flat roof. I was wearing my habit, although no
shoes or veil, and I was worried about the shards of glass at my
feet. I'd just heard planes, but now the sky was clear and all was
silent. Looking out, I could see a city and hills, and beyond the
hills, ocean. It was like an old Dutch painting, all the world
fitted inside its boundaries. I heard a noise and turned. A young
soldier had appeared, alighting onto the roof, and I thought to
run, but something about his movement toward me, his lightness
of step, kept me there. He'd come in friendship. He folded me
into his arms and without a word we stepped off the roof
together. The air strangely held us. I looked back and saw his
shoulders had sprouted immense feathered wings.*

How heavily the soldier flew over the countryside, and how frightened I was he'd let me go. His arms holding me as we wafted toward the sea.

Do I yearn for rescue, then? And what would rescue mean?

2. Benny Finn, Summer, 1974

I used to wish I'd met Isabel first. I imagined it happening at the bakery in Somerville, the one owned by the Polish family, the plump mom with her beehive hairdo handing over huge, sweet pastries covered in powdered sugar, and in the window the fake wedding cake all dusty and cheerful. Or what if I'd met her at Children's Hospital, or at a lunch place near Harvard Square. I had all kinds of scenarios, most of them moving quickly to my apartment, or a much cleaner, nicer version of my apartment, with well-kept gardens or a park outside the windows, instead of scrubby backyards filled with clotheslines and paint peeling from the backs of houses.

But I've stopped that kind of wishing. I'm trying to look at my life honestly this summer. It feels important to do that.

The reality is, I met Isabel over a year ago, March of '73. Liam was a sophomore at Yale, and my mother asked me to bring him up to Milton for spring break. I'd passed through New Haven a few times, on my way to Stamford

to see Mike Saltis, a guy from my unit who lost his legs —
another story — and I'd seen the grayness of the city
buildings on one side, and the grayness of the industrial
crap on the other, but I'd never pulled off the highway
before.

Looking for Liam's address, I kept turning the wrong
way onto one-way streets, seeing signs too late, other cars
whizzing around me like we were all in some ridiculous
race. A couple times, I ended up back on the highway,
heading toward a hospital. I was on my last Camel,
beginning to sweat. It was getting late and rush hour was
starting.

Finally I found the right street. I double-parked at a
big stone archway opening into a courtyard and got out of
the car. Lined up in the dry moat outside some stone walls
were little trees still bare from winter. A crowd of kids
was hanging out, waiting for rides. There was a boy with
Liam's kind of Irish good looks, but this kid had shaggy
black hair almost to his shoulders. Then he waved and
shouted *Benny!* Liam, a hippie.

The girl at his side wore a blue sweater over a long
skirt. Her hair was reddish-gold and curly, done up in a
loose bun. Liam tossed their bags into my trunk, saying,
"Hey, thanks for being only two hours late." Behind us,
cars were honking, but Liam just gave them a peace sign,
shrugging. Then he breezed through the introductions —
"Isabel Howell, Benny Finn" — and Isabel shook my
hand, smiling, and climbed into the back seat. I gave Liam
a look, one of those Brothers Finn faces that meant, *Is*

Mom expecting your girlfriend? He just smiled and clapped me on the shoulder.

I thought Isabel looked shy at first, but she was pretty talkative, actually. By the time we were back on the highway, she'd started asking me questions. What was Somerville like? Did I enjoy my job as an orderly at Children's? How many days off did I get? Liam offered me one of his Marlboros, but I doubted Isabel would like the smoke, so I shook my head. Liam lit one for himself. Then he and Isabel talked a while about one of his papers, on epiphany in a poem about someone's childhood, how it was different from epiphany in *Paradise Lost.*

"It's the difference," Liam said, "between the secular and the divine." Isabel seemed to agree.

By the time we saw the sign for Hammonasset Beach on I-95, Liam was asleep, his temple against the window, and the way he could just conk out like that, practically mid-sentence, reminded me of family beach trips in our old station wagon, me in front playing navigator for Dad, Liam a chubby little kid in back, his head nodding after three blocks. Aidan and Cait could be screeching and fighting — who got the last piece of gum, who saw the first seagull — and there Liam would be, flopped over against the door, hugging a picture book or his stuffed owl, his mouth open like a duck's.

With Liam out, Isabel got quiet. The radio was playing "A Whiter Shade of Pale" — one of the songs my buddy Mike Saltis played nonstop, cooped up in his dad's apartment.

19

I glanced in the rearview, but I couldn't catch Isabel's face, just her shoulder in the blue sweater.

I admit it bothered me when Liam got into Yale. Aidan was at Holy Cross then, and Cait at the University of New Hampshire, but Yale — I don't know. Liam deserved it — he's incredibly smart — but it was like from now on he'd be much higher up on some invisible ladder. I shouldn't have compared myself to him, I know. Easier said than done, though.

I disappointed Mom and Dad not going back to Northeastern after Nam. They're very big on education. Mom grew up in Ireland and only came to this country as a young woman. She went to a small Irish college run by nuns, and to listen to her account of it, she loved every second. Patrick E. Finn, born and bred in Dorchester, worked his proverbial butt off to put himself through Holy Cross, and then (do I hear trumpets?) Harvard Medical School. What's funny is, he spent a year at a seminary, in between college and med school, thinking he'd become a priest. *And I could have done it, Brendan* (my real name, though only my dad uses it, ever since Aidan was little and couldn't say his r's). *I could have done it, only I met your mother that spring and my life was laid out for me. After that I would have made a miserable priest, and that's a fact.* He's a cardiologist now, so he likes to add, *I am still occupied, however, with things of the heart.*

Maybe if I'd switched to an art school or something, I could have hung in there. I used to like to take pictures, and I liked to write too, on my own, but I was pretty out of it in general at Northeastern my freshman and sophomore years. A lot was happening in my life. The whole world was insane then, not that it's sane now, schoolchildren getting killed in Israel, fucking car bombings in Ireland, priests gunned down in Argentina, not to mention Watergate, but still. Five years ago, some fresh and terrible news hit you every hour, mostly from that small country halfway around the globe you'd see on TV, with monks burning themselves up in the streets, or napalmed people running along dirt roads, their skin flayed.

One thing my mother always says, though: *you have to live. No matter what, you live somehow.* It used to surprise me, the way she'd say that. She's a very good person. But she didn't mean you shouldn't care about the terrible things in the world, the blindness and corruption, the wars, just that in spite of it, you do have to get up mornings and pull on your boots, walk across the ice to your classes, get a cup of coffee, visit your Aunt Irene in the hospital, avoid getting your girlfriend pregnant. Who do you help by having a nervous breakdown?

In college I took an English course on recording your life. I wrote down some of the stories Mom always told about her childhood in Ireland, she and her big sister Irene managing chickens in the yard, plus minding about five hundred younger siblings. I wrote about our old priest Father Connaught, a really short man with these cauliflower ears, one of the kindest people I've ever met. And I wrote about the time these white guys in my high school jumped a black kid, Archer, who sat next to me in American History. They broke his nose, the shits, and I heard he almost lost his sight in one eye. They never even got into real trouble for it.

I also wrote about when I was little, waiting for my father at the end of his workday — dark winter afternoons parked with Mom at the station, and me getting so excited to see the train lights coming in the cold. Sitting in the front seat of the car, the babies bundled into the back, you'd hear the whistle a few seconds before the lights broke through the dark. Then came the train, slow and noisy, as big as a church. You'd watch as all the fathers poured out in their hats and long dark coats, holding briefcases, and you'd worry for a minute, was your dad with them or not? Then there he'd be, walking toward the car, looking tired but happy to see you, ready to plant a scratchy kiss first on Mom's cheek and then your own.

I started taking pictures too, for that course. Dad let me borrow his Nikon, which I still have — he finally gave it to me and got a cheaper camera for himself. I shot a lot of stuff down at Cohasset. I really liked the way the houses along the water looked, first in the winter, like sentries holding their own in the cold, then in the spring, blinds peeled back and windows clear, surrounded by green.

I also took a picture of this crazy guy who always wore a hat made of tin foil. I never did learn who he really was.

He might have been a vet, because sometimes he'd wear a piece of camouflage. I kept seeing him around Huntington Ave and occasionally as far up as Copley Square, so I started talking to him one day. We were on the street outside a Greek deli, and I asked him about his hat. He bummed a cigarette off me before answering, like a deal we'd struck. Then, taking little puffs, like sips, he told me the tin foil protected his mind from the gods, who kept trying to send him messages. What messages? I asked. I could have asked, *what gods?* He squinted at me as I took the picture, and then he scuttled away, his silver hat glittering in the sun.

It would be weird going back to college now. Once in a while, though, I think it's possible. The world is full of surprises like that. I picture headlines: *Finn's Triumph.* I picture a press interview, microphones pushed into my face. *So, Mr. Finn, the rumor is you're going to Harvard.* I smile and nod. "Actually, yes, I am." *On a full scholarship?* "Yes, yes, a full one." *And some of your photographs have been bought by the Museum of Fine Arts?* "Yes, just recently they've bought about a hundred." And then I give words of encouragement, meant for all the people out there who have dreams they've let go, like rice thrown at a wedding.

.   .   .

What I never wrote about in that class, or anywhere —
what I couldn't talk about at all — was my girlfriend
Tessa. She got pregnant that spring, five years ago.
Coming from a devout Catholic family a lot like mine, she
knew right away that she couldn't tell them. We kept
hoping the situation would disappear, but by early May it
hadn't, so she went to a doctor her cousin knew about,
who would do the thing illegally, for an amount that
emptied Tessa's and my savings.

I took a lot of pictures of Tessa our sophomore year. She
was naked in some, except for her small silver cross. Most
were black and white, and her hair was almost black anyway, an amazingly deep color. Of course I never showed
my family those photos, but they were my best. Mom
framed some others, including some of Tessa posed with
our family, everyone looking lighthearted, ordinary.

I liked shooting candids the most, like Cait in the
bathroom mirror putting on makeup, her eyes coal-black
around the edges, her lips glossy pink, or my little sister
Eilie, twelve years old, standing by herself on the sand,
looking tight and fierce and shivery, her short hair whip-
ping around her face. One of my favorites was a photo of
Liam reading on the back porch at Cohasset — *The
Collected Poems of W. B. Yeats*, I know it was, though you
can't see the title, you just see him hunched over in shorts
and bare feet, looking like he's deep inside the world of

24

that book. I liked the angle I used on Liam, his face hidden as he bent over those poems.

By the time I got my Army discharge, though, I hardly ever took pictures anymore. The Nikon was in a drawer. I missed it, a little, but I'd lost the urge.

Somewhere around Stonington, Isabel and I started to talk. Leaning toward the front seat, her eyes on mine in the mirror, she asked about our family, how old we all were, how Eilie liked high school. She mentioned she was an only child, which made me feel kind of sorry for her.

Liam must have prepped her a little on life in the Finn household, because she wanted to talk a lot about Catholicism. She said she had a good friend from childhood who became a nun — Helen Barry, her name had been. Isabel had always felt like one of the Barrys, a big Catholic family. Once Helen got on track to becoming Sister Clare, Isabel started visiting her abbey in New Hampshire, Our Lady of the Meadow. A close friend of Helen's became a nun there too, Sister Ines.

"So is that in the cards for you?" I asked.

"What, a nun?" Isabel laughed. "Not likely."

But a few times a year, she said, she would go up and help the Sisters with all kinds of stuff: gardening, making cheese and butter, picking squash, apples, beans — the list went on and on.

"It sounds like paradise!"

"It *is* paradise," she said. "It's a regular earthly paradise."

"I thought Benedictines were cloistered."

"They are."

"You can go inside the cloister?"

"Yes. Well, you can go on the more public part of their land. Sometimes you can go inside the inner Enclosure, like to work in the gardens."

I thought how good that sounded, picking squash and beans in an Enclosure. I pictured going up there with Mike. I doubted he'd go, though.

"It's all so cool to me, how the nuns live," Isabel added. "I grew up Episcopalian."

"Oh, well that explains it," I said.

"Explains what?"

"You weren't raised Catholic! And you definitely did not have nuns for teachers."

"Did you?"

"Oh, yes. Some are unforgettable. Especially Sister Philomena. She'd sneak up on you and swat the back of your neck with a ruler if you even thought about doing mischief."

Isabel was smiling in the rearview. "Well, I don't think these nuns go around with rulers."

"You can't be too careful."

"Advice taken." She put a hand on my headrest, pulling herself forward a bit. "So, do you still consider yourself Catholic?"

I glanced in the mirror. I couldn't tell if her eyes were blue or green — they had this lightness against her dark eyelashes.

"A bad Catholic, yes."

"What makes you bad?"

I couldn't believe this girl was interested in my relationship to the Catholic Church. She was so open, such a listener, and it hit me how little I talked to people about things anymore.

"Well, for one, I haven't gone to Confession in years."

"Why do you have to go to Confession?"

"Christ, just be glad you have to ask that question."

I couldn't say what I was really thinking. I knew that if I started talking to Isabel about the Pope and the Church and celibacy and birth control, before I knew it we'd be on to abortion, and talking calmly on that subject was not my forte.

What I could have told Isabel, though, was that Catholicism was as close to me as my skin — sometimes it itched like crazy. I wasn't like Liam, who could be guilt-free about refusing to go to Confession. It actually bothered me I hadn't gone in so long. When I was a kid, Confession was a very big deal. My list of sins was always growing, like the fungus that could spring up overnight at the edges of our garden. In the dim light of the confessional, though, going over it all with Father Connaught, who smelled like cherry tobacco and who listened calmly and then told me just as calmly what to do for penance, I almost always felt better. I could see how the stuff I'd done was just ordinary, nothing to lose sleep over. I was only human, after all — at least, that was the impression Father Connaught gave me. He was much more forgiving than my actual father.

"So, do you still consider yourself Episcopalian?" I asked Isabel.

"I guess I do."

"Maybe you could keep quiet about that with my mother. You might pass for Irish, and that would make her very happy. A good Irish Catholic girl for her son. Not that Catholic girls are always good!"

She laughed. "It depends on what you mean by good!"

We fell quiet for a while after that, as I negotiated the traffic around Providence and then headed into the Boston outskirts. The radio was playing some Rolling Stones by then, and I really wanted a cigarette. I tried to stop wondering about the color of Isabel's eyes. I started thinking about Dimitri, the little boy I'd met at Children's. He'd died a few days before, leukemia. He liked to write his name over and over again, in different colors. He loved *Sesame Street*, and a few times he said to me, *Hey Benny, look at this, can you watch with me?* Of course I never sat down to watch with him — I couldn't, I was working. But what if I had? What if I'd taken just three minutes to sit in the chair near his bed and watch Bert and Ernie cutting up, or whatever he thought was so hilarious. Why not do something as small as that?

As we pulled into Milton, I thought about Mike Saltis too. For a while now it had been getting harder for me to go see him. It was like visiting a P.O.W. I mean, he *was* a P.O.W. His war was still happening, and he could never talk about much else for very long. We'd chat about Sully sometimes, but never about the day Sully went down.

Saltis owned a lot of books. I got the feeling, though, that he wasn't reading as much as he used to. Mostly he just read the paper. He was still into politics — he'd been very anti-war once he got home, protested in Washington and things like that. He was a bright guy, and in Nam he used to say how he planned to study journalism when he got back to the States. He only needed a few more courses to get his degree, so I don't know what he was waiting for. On good days, he'd open some book of poems and read out loud, and even though I couldn't understand poetry for the life of me, I liked that. You could see how happy it made him, how it got him out of himself.

Saint Brendan the Voyager, he still called me sometimes. In Nam, the first time he called me that, I'd said to him, *Isn't it Saint Brendan the Wanderer?* and he just laughed. *I guess it depends how you look at it, whether you think he got anywhere. He sailed for seven years, didn't he? He found Paradise, for Christ's sake. He brought a whole bunch of monks with him. He rode a whale on Easter.*

By the time we got to Milton, I'd decided to hang around for dinner. The thought of driving to Somerville in the rain, walking into the tired house and then up the stairs to my second-floor apartment, opening the fridge to leftover egg rolls — well, it was a lot nicer to lean against the counter in my mom's clean, dry kitchen with Liam and Isabel, waiting for the chicken to roast. I didn't even mind having to go outside for a smoke. Hunkering under the overhang on the back stoop, I watched the rain come into the light from the windows like tiny silver arrows, pelting the steps and the earthy beds on either side.

Catholic or not, Isabel won over our mother in record time, after the standard polite Maureen Finn grilling session. Liam had gone out with some wild girls in high school, brainy though he was, so when Isabel showed up as the surprise girlfriend, maybe Maureen was too happy to object to her religious status.

Isabel went nuts over our fat mutt Harry, who barked at her insanely for about five minutes before shutting up and lying down with his head on her blue Dr. Scholl's, like she'd conquered him. She scratched Harry's ears. She made Eilie laugh. She helped Mom set the table with the Sunday dishes. She even said she liked the cross-stitch on the kitchen wall — the prayer of Saint Francis. *Lord, make me an instrument of thy peace.* I loved that prayer when I was a kid. I used to look at it while I ate cereal at the kitchen table. *Grant that I may not so much seek to be consoled as to console.* I just really liked the sound of that.

My father's arrival home changed everyone's mood, as usual. Dad is well intentioned, but seeing him walk through the door is like bracing for a test you know you're not prepared for. He's pretty intellectual — maybe he hung out a little too much with the Jesuits. He doesn't always smile too easily, although the smallest hint of one of his smiles goes a long way. He also has a habit of asking questions that owes something to the Spanish Inquisition. Though he's a doctor, the great loves of his life are religion and philosophy — he's always reading books on those subjects and trying to get all of us to read them too, which generally is a waste, although he's been overjoyed to see me reading Saint Augustine's *Confessions* this summer.

So, once we'd all sat down to Mom's chicken and sweet potatoes, and it came out that Isabel was in a course on ethics, Dad brought on the true Patrick Finn charm. He and Isabel got to talking about how various philosophers defined the good. She said her class had been discussing the idea that knowledge of other people could lead to empathy, and empathy could lead to a more peaceful world.

"It's utopian, I know," she said, "but how else does peace start? Doesn't it start inside people, inside their vision of other people? And just think if a country could do that, could see another country as being filled with citizens just like its own."

The idea seemed so great, but also so unrealistic, I couldn't help joining in.

"But how do you get anybody to want to know anybody else?" I said. "I mean, it seems like most people don't give a — really couldn't care less whether they know anyone right around them, forget about understanding other countries. You look at all these vets — who cares what happened to them?"

Dad shook his head in that slow, deliberate way of his that can make you crazy. "Well, Brendan, I don't know—"

I'd had this discussion with him before, and I knew he thought I was exaggerating.

"You wear a uniform, walk on the street, people look away, Dad. They look away."

"I think Benny's right," said Isabel. Her eyes met mine with such clarity and directness. "I think you're right, Benny. That kind of understanding is never easy."

I almost forgot the argument. I had the ridiculous, sharp urge to leap across the table and kiss this girl, this Isabel Howell. Instead I jumped up and took the water pitcher into the kitchen.

For a minute or two, I bent over the sink just letting the cold water overflow the pitcher's rim. I couldn't go right back. I knew my family would be exchanging looks, like *What in Christ's name is wrong with him* now*? They loved me, I knew, and I was lucky to have them. But sometimes you have to face how isolated you are, moving somewhere outside the world of your family and other people you care about. And then, practically from nowhere, here comes this beautiful ambassador crossing the boundary in a matter of hours. How do you answer to that?

Soon I could hear Mom redirecting the conversation: "Patrick, how was your day?" Sure enough, Dad started to hold court, describing some tricky case involving a cardiac bypass.

By the time I came back with the water, Isabel was thanking Mom for the dinner, and Liam was bringing their coats from the hall.

"You'll miss dessert," Mom said. "Where will you go, in the rain?"

Liam threw on his jacket. "I want to show Isabel a little of Milton, in all its wet glory. Benny, could we borrow your car?"

I tossed him the keys.

Mom sighed as the front door closed behind them. Patrick gave her a reassuring smile, absentmindedly brushing crumbs off the table for Harry to lick up.

I kept thinking, helping Eilie wash the dishes and then walking Harry around the block, smoking while I waited for him to sniff every bush and leave his message on each and every leaf and blade of grass (*Harry was here!*) — I kept thinking how lucky Liam was, to have someone like Isabel in his life. I hoped he would deserve her, and treat her well.

I brought Harry back home, and then I walked in the rain all the way to this bar where I used to stop in sometimes, and sitting in the dark, watching some mindless stuff on TV, I must have drunk a shitload, because the next thing I remember is cracking my toe on the wheelbarrow in the back garden trying to find the steps, then banging on the kitchen door because Liam had my keys. Mom came to peer out the window in her old bathrobe, her face scrubbed for bed. She looked worried at first, and then — once I came inside — disgusted and really sad. But I couldn't do much to reassure her right then, because the kitchen was bending, the linoleum slippery and soft as a rice paddy. I sank down to my butt and sat there for a sec, my pants soaked, my back against the cabinets, trying not to look at her while she got some some coffee going and then a cup of Tetley's for herself. It seemed to take her a long time, and I just hoped she wouldn't start talking. I'd lost my Camels somewhere. I couldn't stop thinking about a smoke, but I knew that if I moved I'd throw up, and in any case Maureen would toss the pack in the trash if I tried to light up inside.

The coffee, when it finally came, was hot and bitter. Mom sat at the kitchen table then, her face tight with disappointment and exhaustion, stirring a teaspoon of sugar into her tea and milk. Over her shoulder I read the cross-stitch: *Grant that I may not so much seek to be consoled as to console, to be understood, as to understand.*

Mom looked old, without her lipstick or earrings, just her wedding ring with the small diamond.

to be loved, as to love

She pulled her bathrobe tighter and I could tell she was trying not to cry.

"I don't know how to help you, Benny. I really have no idea. I don't know what is going to happen to you."

3. Sister Clare

This looks as if it will be a spectacular day, so much drier than it's been. Saturday, the first of June — Pentecost tomorrow. The sky is already the lightest blue.

The bathroom is crowded, as usual, both showers in use, and I have just a minute to wash my face. Rushing to morning prayers, I catch the fragrance of jasmine in the hanging bowl by the church's back entrance — Mother Heloise's favorite flower.

A dream is lingering — Isabel was in it, and, I think, a soldier again. Someone was missing, or hurt. A child, or possibly a calf. The Community had to barricade our church doors, but I ran outside to help. How terrible the world can be.

As I join the Community for Lauds, the dream starts to erase itself, and this new day begins.

Singing the psalms, I remember that Isabel will be coming to visit. She says she'll be here for lunch — I hope so! She's a bit cavalier about time.

A huge day, yesterday, filled with cooking for the Feast of the Visitation — bouillabaisse. The leftovers will be good for today's lunch. And tomorrow, if the weather holds, we'll have a festive picnic outdoors, and Father Julian will bless the fields right there. Sister Ines's family has given us fresh strawberries in honor of the day. She entered at Pentecost, a few months before I did.

I try to focus on our singing, but instead I go over the list of things I have to do. How to squeeze it all in: watering the flower beds; weeding; helping plant beans, if I can; planning out my Latin lessons for the Postulants (and how I can keep even one step ahead of them, I have no idea); meeting with a young college student living in the guesthouse this summer; talking with Sister Marina and Mother Christina Joseph, if we can catch her, to go over the picnic tomorrow. My parlor with Isabel will be a chance simply to sit and enjoy her presence.

Fled forever, I feel, are the poems and stories I thought I would write. Sometimes I catch a wisp of a notion, like a feather falling out of the sky, but it floats off the next instant. Mother Heloise encourages me to write in my daybook. She says she tries to jot down ideas for her paintings in the small sketchbooks she carries in her pocket.

"You have to stay prepared," she says, "in this as in all things, Sister Clare. One day you may find a surprising half hour of freedom in your day, and a poem will be ready to write."

It's almost comical to realize how much free time people think nuns have. I'm so busy here. My time is just not my own.

. . .

I have to say, we sound like a sorry bunch this morning.
Sister Clement is coughing — allergies. Sister Ines looks
as if she's a thousand miles away, and I wonder if she's
worried about something. I miss being able to talk with
her at leisure. Even Mother Abbess's voice sounds husky
and out of tune; she has just lost her brother to a heart
attack.

After our first two psalms, though, I begin to feel com-
forted and buoyed up, as I have the feeling I often do,
especially at Lauds and Prime, of swimming — stroke
after stroke, held up by the water. Beauty and power fill
the lines of these chants. I cherish the sound of the Latin,
the simplicity of the melody. If we're swimming together,
as one body, one voice, no matter what, we will be all
right. "Make love, not war" could be about the chant too.

A familiar memory comes to me on the tide of an anti-
phon: one morning, years ago, when Isabel was seven, she
found me at the lake by my house, swimming in my
birthday suit. It was the week before my first year of high
school began, so I must have just turned fourteen. Her
mother was in the hospital, the last stages of ovarian
cancer. Isabel sat on the big rock, waiting for me to come
back to shore. "Bring me my towel," I said to her, and she
brought it as I climbed naked onto the rock. "Is it your
mother," I said, "has she gone?" and she nodded, begin-

ning to cry. I held her for a few minutes, as we sat on that rock together, the towel around me, and then I walked with her up through the meadow to my house, to call her poor distraught dad and let him know she was all right.

Isabel has gone through so much. Sometimes I feel more like her older sister than her friend. Sometimes I even feel like a mother. She thinks of me as so strong, and so confident of my goals.

But how unlike that I am, especially now, up again and down again, up and down — grateful and excited one minute, as I go toward my First Vows, tremendously anxious the next. Almost three years I have been in this Novitiate, and the question of my next step comes closer and closer. Will I do this? Will I really make this Commitment? This morning it feels as if I'm still just playing on the shore, but I worry that to take these vows will be like walking onto a boat and leaving so many people I've loved, as the boat carries me to another country.

Mother Heloise nods sagely whenever I talk this way. She has an Italian accent I love — she's from Ravenna.

"Yes, well, Sister Clare, you're right about the enormity of such a Commitment. No one promised it would be easy."

I nod and say I know, but inwardly I want to tear off my habit, kick it right out the window, and shout, *Why in God's name should I do this, then? What is the point? I'm not cut out for this, not at all! I could be free; I could walk out of here right now, and have an ordinary life.*

38

I gaze at Mother Heloise's sharp and lovely face, each wrinkle familiar, each facet of her smile. She knows exactly what I'm thinking, in spite of my outward diplomacy.

"It is not simple, to be always part of a Community," she says. "One often feels, especially at first, is this really what I signed up for? Where is the glory? And what is all this, with the getting up at all hours and praying seven times a day, and once at Matins? And why do nuns not have holidays?" She contemplates my face. "I will say, however, Sister Clare, that you will not be leaving anyone behind. The love you already have inside you will simply grow. But then, I am not telling you news."

At this, I have to smile. When I first entered, she would give me encouragement, but at the beginning I thought I had so much courage I could have spared some for a dozen other novices. I couldn't yet know what she knew. I envisioned being a bride in each moment of each day, chaste and rapturous, caught up into some constant, glorious consummation with God. I could not imagine the days and weeks that have often opened out in their emptiness around me. If Christ is the bridegroom, He can be an incredibly absent one. As Mother Heloise likes to say, "It is true, He does often appear to keep a lady waiting."

But of course I know, when I think God is hiding from me, couldn't I be the hidden one? And yet how do you become present to something you can't even sense some days, not even in your littlest toe? So often lately, I can't help my despair.

"Why look so far away for God, though?" Mother Heloise asks. "Look to the person you sing next to — look to the Sister you make lunch with, or pull weeds with. Look to a guest who comes, searching for something here. Is God so very distant?"

In the midst of our prayers, I am lifted. Something is here. It must be. May I hold to it. May I contribute to it.

4. The Hidden Boy

The morning Isabel was supposed to catch her bus up to
New Hampshire for the second half of her spring break, I
came by the house. I'd told Dad I'd help with the spring
cleanup on the yard. He'd run to the store for a new rake
and mulch. Liam, always the late riser, was still in the
shower, and Mom was busy out back inspecting the Lily
of the Valleys that had come up by the kitchen steps, so I
ended up chatting with Isabel in the kitchen. Eilie was
playing "You're So Vain" upstairs. Other than that, and
the shower running, the house was quiet. A few breakfast
dishes lay unwashed in the sink.

Isabel had told Liam how much she liked the photo of
him reading, and he told her I'd taken it.

"Could you show me some more?"

"Oh, God, they're nothing special."

"Liam said your mom has some here, you'd know
where."

It felt idiotic to make excuses, so I went into the living
room to look in Mom's desk, in the drawer where she kept
a lot of photos she intended to frame one day. It turned
out she had a couple in there from Nam, which surprised

me. As I listened to Isabel washing dishes, I looked at a black and white of Mike Saltis cleaning his rifle, hair falling into his eyes. Bare-chested and skinny, he had a medal around his neck that you couldn't see all that well, but I knew it was his oval medal of Saint Michael with wings, slaying the dragon.

I looked at one of Sully, who was this very laid-back guy from Bridgeport. In the photo he's holding his boot upside down and laughing, a joint dangling out of the corner of his mouth, and he looks like any nineteen-year-old black guy who happens to be sitting in the jungle. The photo was clear and right, but I knew it was just a wish now, because I had this other picture in my head, of Sully's body after he went down. The real picture was the one I never actually took, and because it was inside me and not on paper somewhere, there was no tearing it up or forgetting about it.

I chose to show Isabel a few photos I shot during the first weeks after my discharge, before I put the camera away for good. One is of a little boy hiding in a bush. You can look a long time and not notice him, but once you see his sneakers, his hand, a bit of his face, the whole picture changes. I don't think I thought too much about the boy when I shot the photo, and I'm not even sure whose kid he was — my neighborhood is full of them. It's kind of mysterious, though, how he's just there, whether you see him or not.

Isabel quickly dried her hands, and looked at the shots one by one. I couldn't have known how awkward that would feel. Ordinarily, nobody outside my family saw my photographs. She stood by the counter, silent, looking at them with a kind of — I don't know, tenderness, I'd almost say. She spent the longest on the last one, the kid in the bush.

"I like this one especially."

"Thanks."

"You have a real eye."

I laughed a little. I liked my photos well enough, but I had no illusions about them. I took those pictures because I wanted to.

Just then Liam bounded into the kitchen with Isabel's duffel bag, hair still wet from his shower. He stopped for a second, looking at Isabel, my pictures in her hands. Then he bustled out through the dining room, tossing words over his shoulder as he went.

"Your bus leaves in an hour, Isa, let's go."

"An hour?" said Isabel. "Yikes!" And she started to hurry after him. In the doorway she paused, though, spinning back to hand me the pictures, and I was surprised to see her blush.

"Thanks for showing me, Benny," she said, and then in a flash she was laughing on the front stoop, saying her goodbyes to Mom and Eilie, to the house, and to crazy Harry, lovesick and upset to see her on her way.

It was a relief when Isabel left, to be honest. I doubted I'd see her again, the way Liam was, and that was fine.

. . .

That summer our family was mostly down at Cohasset. My father put up with the extra-long train ride from Boston each day so he could breathe some sea air and sport his old-man sandals with white socks, those and his khaki shorts, spattered with paint from one house project or another. On weekends I knew he played rounds of windy badminton with Eilie, grilled swordfish, walked on the beach with Mom, looked for shells to place along the windowsills. They'd both gotten older. Sometimes, in the late afternoon, if the tide was right, he dug for clams with Cait, who still had a summer job in Cohasset like Liam and I used to do. Aidan taught sailing lessons in summer, in Hingham, and worked in a community recreations office in winter.

Liam had landed a job doing research for a history professor at Harvard. He was staying at the house in Milton — or supposed to be. Our mother liked the idea of one family member at home, to discourage all the robbers just waiting their chance *(Looks like the Finns are off, let's grab their flatware, or how about that very fine hand-crocheted tea cozy?)*. She had asked Liam and me to do some upkeep — weeding, clipping the hedges, cleaning out the garage, planting some annuals around the daylilies in front, fertilizing and cutting the roses.

I went over a couple times a week, after work. Liam was pretty much MIA, but I liked having that garden to myself. Planting thyme between the stepping stones in back, mowing the lawn, listening to the comfortable evening hush of that neighborhood, I could almost be part of the garden, not a person even, just something living and breathing the loamy air.

It was gardening work, actually, that had kept me alive, the spring of '71. I'd been pretty fucked up since my discharge almost a year before, living at home, barely able to hoist myself out of bed, much less out of the house. I got a few small jobs on construction crews, I worked the register at a gas station for a while, but I'd always quit after a week or two and retreat to the room that used to be Aidan's, at the back of the house. My room over the garage got claimed by Eilie and Liam as their hangout space while I was in Nam, and I didn't care enough to push them out. All of Aidan's old sailing trophies were still in his room, and this dark blue wallpaper that made you feel like you were underwater.

Maureen Finn became determined to pry me loose, like some six-foot-three barnacle that she could see she might have stuck to her forever. One of my Uncle Leo's friends owned a landscape company. She drove me to an interview. The owner Mr. Gottschalk was a nice guy, and one of his own sons was just shipping out to Nam.

At first I could hardly get through a morning's work — hauling mulch, planting trees, doing cleanup — but Mr. Gottschalk was good about letting me ease into a full-day schedule. I started to look forward to those hours outdoors, in spite of hangovers or pure exhaustion. I liked how your mind could lighten after a while, how you could get out of thinking. You'd stop expecting the dead body on the other side of a hedge, stop listening for rifle fire. You could go for hours without saying goodbye to the world. All you'd need to know would be right in front of you: daylight, weeds, worms making their steady way through earth.

After a few of my yard work evenings in Milton I could tell Liam wasn't staying there much at all. He'd started clipping the hedge, but never finished. He watered the grass, but only sometimes. In the house, his plates and glasses stood piled in the sink, and mice got into the cupboard where he left food in the trash for who knows how many days.

I finally ran into him one night in July as I came by to water the garden. The sky was still a peaceful light blue, the shadows sharp on the lawn. It was an amazingly clear day, a day like you get maybe once all summer. The shadier parts of the yard were cool and damp. The white impatiens looked as bright as stars.

I bummed a cigarette — I was trying to quit — and asked him how his job was going. He said the research was interesting, about The Irish War of Independence. He thought he might do his thesis on that subject in a couple of years. Then he confessed that he was living in Cambridge with Isabel and a few friends from Yale. They were still together. He said she had a job at a nursing home. Their apartment was on the third floor of an old commercial building on Mass Ave, quite a few blocks up from Harvard Square. Isabel was doing a lot of painting lately, he said, on her days off.

"I didn't know she painted," I said.

Liam shrugged. He thanked me for taking care of the lawn. I could tell he was worried about Mom finding out he and Isabel had moved in together. She thought the world of Isabel, but she's very strict about that kind of thing.

Liam called the next morning to see if he could borrow my car that weekend. He wanted to go up to Gloucester with Isabel. So that Saturday I found the apartment on Mass Ave. It was a fairly cruddy place right over a bar, which was next to a launderette and a Dunkin' Donuts, but Isabel had done up their room nicely, with rows of her watercolors clipped to pieces of string, like clothes on a clothesline. It looked like she did picture after picture of the same thing, only in a different light, so the colors would change. Some were of Mass Ave from their window. Some were of the bed — really just a mattress on the floor. All those squares and rectangles of color floated together, like parts of a bigger picture that had no sides but just sailed into the world.

Liam had dozens of books on some shelves, and on top of the shelves sat a jar with paintbrushes in it, tubes of paint, dental floss, Zig Zags, a hair brush, a half-filled ash tray, and a picture someone had taken of Isabel on Liam's lap, where you couldn't see her face, only Liam's, as he held her and laughed. Liam's mascot, a foot-high blue plastic Mister Peanut, stood on the floor beside the bed, and his Red Sox cap hung on the wall above it, next to that poster you see everywhere, of nudes dancing in a circle against a blue background.

Isabel was at the stove making pancakes. She was in a loose sundress, standing barefoot on the dusky red linoleum. The housemates — two girls — wandered in looking sleepy, and one of them brewed some coffee while Isabel started to sing bits of some Irish songs an old lady in the nursing home had taught her. Most of the songs I knew from Nana, and I was sure Liam did too, though he claimed not to. Isabel's favorite was the one that begins, *I'll tell my ma when I go home, the boys won't leave the girls alone*, and ends, *Let them all come as they will, for it's Albert Mooney she loves still.*

That morning was nice, with the songs and the pancakes, but I realized I embarrassed Liam in front of those Yale kids. It pissed me off, but I understood too: I was older, and what was I doing with my life? Maybe I was also a big glaring reminder to Liam of where he'd come from — the tidy neighborhoods of Milton, the Finns of Dorchester and the Horns of County Cork. I think, on some level, he wanted to start fresh, to get free of history, which was ironic, considering his major.

My having been in the Army didn't help either. I doubted many Yale kids would have joined even if they'd been called up. I'd known a lot of guys in college who got deferments for fake psychiatric problems, and one of my friends got CO status. Most people I knew thought I was crazy not to try for a student deferment, at least. Liam, the day he found out I'd been drafted and didn't plan to get out of it, shouted in my face that I was an idiot, the War was obscene, I was going to die, and all for nothing.

Over pancakes that day, it came out that Isabel's nursing home was clear over on Commonwealth Avenue. Every morning she had to get up at five to take a bus and two subways. It sounded like the place was pretty much on my way to the hospital, so I told her she could ride mornings with me. She waved me off and said she was fine. A few days later, though, she called me up.

"Benny, about that ride to work."

I see my offer more clearly now. I wasn't too clear then. Well, I had moments of clarity — as Dad used to say, in the midst of all the chaos of children and dogs, *Could we strive for a moment of clarity here?*

I enjoyed Isabel's company — I thought it was as simple as that. I was on my own a lot then. Most of my friends from Northeastern had moved away, some were in graduate school. One of the few friends I still saw was Mike, but I didn't know how to help him anymore. He got into very dark moods, with his body like that. What do you do with that kind of loneliness? Someone could have loved him, though, right? — no matter about his legs. He was a good-looking guy, and very generous. He was

49

always giving things away. He gave me a book of poems by Gerard Manley Hopkins, which he'd won as a prize in college. He'd hand you anything he thought had value. I realize now he had a lot on his mind he never talked about.

In any case, I got closer to Isabel, talking in the car on hot mornings, rainy mornings, crammed up against all the belligerent drivers honking or plunging out of side streets right in front of us, never looking. Everyone in a big hurry to get to work, and all I wanted was to stay in that traffic, just talking to this girl, just having her there with me in my little VW. It's not that I was hoping for anything. Or if I hoped, I tried to ignore it. If I had known Sister Clare then, or someone like her — though no one is like her — I could have figured it out, maybe. I could have gotten some advice — how to balance myself, how to rise out of the situation, have some backbone — leave Isabel alone. Let's just say I was like someone who doesn't know how to sail a boat, but who can't stay off the water.

One day we'd just pulled up to the nursing home when Isabel told me how her mother died early one morning in a hospital, while Isabel, seven years old, was sound asleep at home. Someone woke her up to tell her, she couldn't remember who, her dad was at the hospital, and once she'd heard, she ran away. Not telling anyone, she ran to the Barrys' beach to find Helen — Sister Clare. She still couldn't forgive herself, she told me.

"For what?"

Isabel looked surprised. "For being asleep."

"Maybe your mom wanted it that way. Maybe she hoped to spare you."

I saw she'd started to cry. She'd opened her door and already had one foot outside the car.

"You just know when you've failed somebody. Forever, you just know."

"You were seven years old, Isabel, for Christ's sake."

For a minute she looked at me, saying nothing. I forgot about the traffic, my job, the hour. I wished I could give her something to take into her day, to hold against that memory.

"You know what Eilie used to say? She used to say, *I think God made the world, and Mother Nature made the trees.* I loved that. I loved the way she made it all sound so balanced and right, like God and Mother Nature were such a fabulous team, you know? The thing is, they really fuck up sometimes. I mean, it's hard to understand why things happen the way they do."

Isabel hung there in the open door, still halfway out of the car, breathing deep against her tears. I didn't know what else to say. Sometimes you can only look at a person, do your best to hold their face in your mind, like you're storing them up for the future.

"Thanks, Benny."

For a minute I thought she might say something more, but instead she just got out and shut the door. I watched her walking quickly into the building.

．　．　．

Another morning, a little while later, Isabel pulled from her purse a small packet wrapped in wax paper. The paper had a small stamp on it, a fleur-de-lys. It was a wedge of cheese, she said, from the abbey she visited in New Hampshire. She'd just been up there a day or two.

She held the wedge in her lap while I drove. The traffic was heavy.

"What's it like up there?" I said. "How do you spend your time?"

"Well, you do a lot of thinking," she said.

I turned to look at her, stopped by yet one more red light.

"How do you go about it?"

"What?"

"I mean, how is it different to think up there? Do you sit in a special chair and concentrate?"

Isabel laughed. "Yes, I sit in the Thinking Chair. It's right next to the Feeling Chair."

"Right, sorry," I said. "You know how I am about nuns."

The light turned green. We followed the long line across the bridge.

"No, I — it's hard to explain, Benny."

"Actually, maybe I could use a Thinking Chair myself. Or better, let the nuns do my thinking for me. Could be they're more cut out for it."

Isabel shook her head. "No one can think for you, that's the thing."

She pulled off a little piece of the cheese.

"Anyway, open up."

I glanced over, both hands on the wheel, then opened my mouth and she placed the cheese on my tongue, like a pill she was ordering me to take, or a wafer. The cheese was musky and rich. You could almost taste the grasses in it, that the cows had grazed on.

"It's good, thanks. I don't know if it's worth being a nun to make it, though."

Isabel scoffed. "I think it's a good life."

I just shrugged.

"You confuse me, Benny. You said yourself it sounded like paradise."

"I did?"

"Yes, the day I met you. The first time I told you how I visit up there sometimes."

"OK," I said. "Paradise, minus a few things."

"Like minus what?"

"Well, sex for one."

She rolled her eyes. "What if you like sex, but you also love other things?"

"Such as?"

"Oh, I don't know — like God?"

"See though, that's the same old Catholic bullshit. Sorry, Isabel, but as the only Catholic in this car I've got to point this out. Can't you love God, and also like sex once in a while?"

"You sound just like Liam! I thought you really liked that priest, what's his name?"

"Father Connaught?"

"Do you think he was unhappy?"

"That's not a fair question."

"Why not?"

"I don't know." I shrugged, as I thought about Father Connaught's smile, shaking everyone's hand after Mass. "Maybe he would've been even happier with a woman in his bed."

"Just in his bed?"

I turned onto Comm Ave.

"You're right, not just in bed. You can do it anywhere."

Isabel threw her hands in the air, but I was glad to see her laughing. "You're hopeless! Don't you think a priest like Father Connaught might feel really close to some women in a deep, Platonic way? Who's to say sex makes for the all-time best relationships?"

"Boy, Isabel, you're full of surprises. You sound like a walking advertisement for celibacy. What does Liam make of that?"

She was still smiling, but her eyes looked sad. There were shadows under them, like she hadn't been getting enough sleep.

"I'm not saying it's for everyone. Probably not for you, Benny!"

Isabel had no idea how little sex I'd had since Tessa. My part in the conversation was silly, given that fact. I can't say I wanted to set her straight, though. I'm sure she imagined me leading an ordinary life filled with relationships. That summer I never thought of my isolation as a choice I was making, but maybe it was. I was frightened, I admit. Loneliness can be a kind of shelter.

"One of the abbey cows was about to give birth," Isabel said. "I hoped it would happen over the weekend. The nuns thought so, but by the time I left there was still no calf."

"I like calves," I said. "It's just the whole life that sounds like misery to me."

"Well, to me it sounds pretty good."

Isabel's voice had gotten softer. And the way she said that, it occurred to me, what if those nuns do have it all figured out? Cows and meadows, farm work, gardening, long days of quiet, people all around you who completely understand what your life is like? — couldn't that help you feel more human?

Isabel seemed to get preoccupied changing radio stations, and by the time she found a classical one she liked, with two voices singing in harmony, a man and woman — "Oh, Mozart!" she said. "I think this is from *The Magic Flute*." — we'd arrived at the nursing home. We'd barely made it in time, but she stayed in the car a minute, and the song floated in the air around us, making my chest hurt. I kept it on as I pulled back into traffic and headed to the hospital.

. . .

The next morning was humid. Somehow I got to telling Isabel a little about Tessa, how she lived in Concord now, married, with a baby, but about the farthest I took the story was to say, sometimes you look back at things and can't believe your own carelessness.

Maybe I would have told more, had Isabel asked. Our talks had been getting kind of frank, after all. I could have trusted her with the rest of it: the abortion, and how afterward Tessa built a moat around herself, and maybe I did too. We stayed together, but it wasn't the same, I couldn't figure out how to get back to her.

Isabel didn't ask me, though. She seemed tired, wiping her forehead in the humidity.

That afternoon, I was dripping sweat in the air conditioning, wheeling a little girl to radiology, when I got a call. It was Isabel. She said she'd been trying to reach Liam at Widener Library. She said she really wanted to go home early, but she'd forgotten her key.

"Are you OK, Isabel?"

"I'm fine, really, just tired."

"Actually, I have one of your keys. Liam gave it to me a few weeks ago, just in case." I waited for her to say something. I looked at my watch. "I could get off early for lunch. I could come get you, take you home."

"Could you?"

She sounded far away, but grateful. When I hung up, I saw my hands were shaking.

. . .

Outside the hospital, the heavy air plastered my cotton shirt to my back. The dusty city trees waited for a breeze. I could practically see the car exhaust, a thick afternoon haze.

Twenty minutes later I stood at the front station of Isabel's nursing home. Around the corner was a big common room with a TV blasting and a lot of old people strapped into chairs or wheelchairs, staring at nothing. Some game show was on, horns blowing and people clapping, but even the people facing the TV weren't really looking at it. Some of their heads drooped clear to their sorry chests. Not one of them held a book, a newspaper, even a potholder-maker. Nana crossed my mind, how slowly she walked, but how she read mysteries and cooked each day in her own house with my Aunt Irene.

Isabel came to the station still looking tired. In spite of the heat, she was wearing a white sweater over her light blue uniform. Inside the hot car, I rolled down my window and she took off the sweater. I leaned over to roll her window down too, and realized she was starting to cry. I scrounged some Kleenex from my back seat.

"You OK?"

She started wiping her eyes, her black eye makeup blotting the Kleenex. It occurred to me that maybe she and Liam were fighting.

"I'm just upset," she said.

I waited. I was hurting bad for a cigarette, but I still wanted to quit, and I'd gotten down to about five a day.

"Remember," Isabel said, "I told you about the old lady who liked to sing the Irish songs?"

"Uh-huh."

"She died. She was there yesterday. I brushed her hair and clipped her nails, and while I was clipping she started to sing that song — what was it?"

"The one about Albert Mooney?"

"Yes." She laughed a little. "Albert Mooney she loves still."

"That's a good song."

She was twisting a Kleenex around and around her finger. "And you know what really got to me, Benny? When one of the nurses told me she'd died, I went to her room, thinking maybe I could at least see her body. But her bed was stripped bare. She'd had this pretty quilt, and a couple of teacups in saucers. There was nothing left."

We sat in the car's heat, Isabel sobbing. A lot of people were walking past on their lunch hour.

"It was like she'd never been in her room at all. I know people die, but—"

I waited for her, the keys bunched up in my lap, holding off the huge urge to wrap her in my arms, pull her to me. I looked out the window, trying to distract myself watching the traffic, but then her hand was on my arm. She was thanking me, coming closer, and then she kissed me on the cheek, near my mouth.

I can't tell you what Isabel meant by that kiss. I didn't wait to think about it, honestly. Before I knew it my arms were around her, who cared who was walking by in the summer heat. I barely thought about Liam. My hand on her thigh, my mouth on hers, she fell into me completely. Unbelievable, to press her so close across the stupid gearshift, to feel her open to me that way.

Over her shoulder, I saw some girls walking by, a guy with a briefcase, so normal, and it woke me up. I tried to get a hold of myself, kissing her neck, her mouth, the delicate place just under her ear, but drawing back. Finally we moved apart. I buttoned one of her buttons, and she smoothed my hair, her fingers pausing a few seconds at my mouth. It was all I could do not to start again. Somehow I started the car instead.

With my hands glued to the steering wheel, I got the first black wave of guilt. I still felt high, though, too, with Isabel next to me, and everything else — the people on the sidewalks, the other cars — it all looked bright and hazy and far away, the way the mainland can look as your ferry leaves it in a gauzy heat spell. I couldn't stop glancing over at her, her face, her hair, the half-inch of her cinnamon-colored bra still showing under her uniform, the soft roundness of the edges of her breasts, her hands now in her lap. I was drunk, but not like it ever felt, drinking.

.   .   .

59

Trying to cross the Charles, heading over to Cambridge, we got stuck in midday traffic. I wondered where all those cars were headed at that hour. The whole thing — gridlock, work, crossing bridges only to cross back again, getting up, going to sleep, dying in nursing homes or hospitals — all of it seemed like part of some great unthinking ritual you get caught up in. We idled there in the heat, a little breeze puffing humid air into our faces, a salt-marsh smell. Sweat trickled down the back of my neck into my shirt. I could taste Isabel's tongue. My cheek was stinging, and in the mirror I could see a cut near my eye — how it got there, I didn't know.

The Charles was glittering and blue, seagulls floating overhead, and down in the current a scull with two rowers moving straight and fast. I started humming that song, thinking the words. *Albert Mooney says he loves her, all the boys are fighting for her.*

"Benny, listen—"

I watched a young seagull hanging in one place, almost motionless. I stopped humming, but I could still hear the song. *Let them all come as they will, for it's Albert Mooney she loves still.*

A drop of sweat slid behind my ear.

"No, Isabel. It's OK."

"I'm sorry."

"I know. I'm sorry too."

"I was just so grateful to you, for listening."

"It's OK. Forget about it."

Some cars around me started to honk, as if honking was a way of getting somewhere. Isabel was looking out the window, at her side mirror.

She turned then, and I caught her eyes. She said, "I have to tell you something."

In the seconds before she said it, I suddenly knew. It was like, I'd *known. Wait!* I wanted to shout. But I knew she couldn't wait. I looked at the car in front of us, a little white Datsun with a dent in the tail. A girl was turning around to hand a bottle to a kid in the back seat. You could hear the kid crying.

Isabel's hand was resting on my arm. I wondered how old the mother was, how the car had gotten dented.

"Benny, I think I'm pregnant."

I can still see us in traffic, midday, bumper to bumper on that bridge over the Charles. My VW is this little red shell in the midst of all these other shells, blue and yellow and white, all with soft humans inside, and it's like some god comes stomping along and takes a big snapshot — an Instamatic — of Isabel's flushed face, her cinnamon bra, the floating gulls, the lit-up water, the milky blue sky, and then tosses the snapshot into my lap like a song, saying, *Look! Here it is. Here's something important. Now figure it out.*

5. Sister Clare

Mother Rita finds me in the herb garden to say that Isabel has arrived. I'm showing our guest Anna a bit of the Enclosure, before she starts helping Sister Clement with the beans. Our dog Laude is loping across the near meadow, probably in search of Father Julian.

Isabel has missed lunch, alas, so I ask permission to bring her a slice of lemon cake and a glass of iced tea. Luckily, in the kitchen, I see Sister Marina. She wipes her forehead with a handkerchief, and stuffs it back into her sleeve.

"Ah! Sister Clare. Mother Abbess has given the go-ahead on our picnic tomorrow, for Pentecost. The weather looks good. Will you still be able to meet at two, or could we just take a moment now?"

"Well," I say, thinking of Isabel. "If we can be quick."

We go over the menu, and she writes down a list of questions for Mother Christina Joseph, our Cellarer. Sister Marina says Father Julian is asking a couple of young guests to help bring the picnic tables out to the shady area beside the peach orchard. Mother Heloise is hoping I'll help her cut flowers for the tables.

I'm worried Isabel will give up on me. I run to the parlor, but when I knock and enter, I see that it's empty. Mother Rita has given us the smallest one. A window looks out onto the raggedy patch of lawn by the driveway, surrounded by ivy beds and impatiens and a few cosmos. Craning my neck, I glimpse the purple irises too, which I helped to plant before I entered.

When I hear Isabel's light knock, I call out, "*Benedicamus domino.*"

Isabel comes in with a soft "*Deo Gratias.*" I put my hands through the pine grille, and she holds them tight as we kiss. She's in a sundress, her hair pulled off her neck in the heat.

I pass her the cake and tea and she's very grateful. As she eats, she tells me about the mice commandeering the little house she's renting this summer at home. She says she's had the chance to go swimming a few times at the lake, although the water's still icy. A snapping turtle has been spotted on the lakeside near the Houghtons' property and everyone is worried about it.

While she talks, I have the sensation of walking right through the grille, its slats vaporized into thin air. My white wimple and veil vanish, my habit, scapular, and belt, my black sneakers — much too hot on a day like today. I am naked a moment, and then, magically, I'm in ordinary clothes — a light cotton top, a short skirt, bare legs.

Couldn't this happen, after all? I could walk out of the parlor, my hair free in the warm air. We'd jump into Isabel's car and drive home, radio blasting. I'd walk into my family's kitchen. I'd have Dad's hamburgers for dinner, hot off the grill, or I'd go with Mattie or one of my brothers to one of the restaurants in town. I'd taste Mom's scones and tea. I'd drink champagne. I'd have my hair cut fashionably. I'd begin to think about the rest of my life, in the great open world. What poems could I write? Who might I fall in love with? Where could I travel? Ireland or Italy? Japan? Peru? Just to walk through my family's meadow, down to the lake again, my bare knees brushing Queen Anne's Lace, daisies, Bachelor's Buttons. The great bowl of water would be cold, open and rippling, ready for my plunge.

As Isabel talks about her worries, though, I feel new gratitude for my life here. To have this Community — to have the day's architecture of the office, the year's architecture — something about this order, this grace, can give me a sense of rising out of myself. I feel part of something much greater than any one of us, something human and sacred. Anchored here, I have the chance to offer something to the world in a more constant way, don't I? I can begin this minute, with a good word.

"I think you're doing beautifully, Isabel."

Her mascara is starting to run, as her earrings tremble.

"But I feel so — directionless — right now. It's like I'm stuck in some stupid marsh."

I think of her, a little girl, holding out the towel for me on the rock. I sat there with her until her sobs grew quiet, and she and I contemplated my neighbor old Mr. Dunbar as he rowed across the lake in front of us, his canvas fishing hat rakishly cocked on his white head.

"You'll find your way, Isa, I know you will."

"How? How did *you* find your way?"

"I *didn't*, for the longest time."

"But you're here!"

I laugh. "Yes, I'm here."

I could say more. I could say sometimes you are yourself chosen, against your will, by something greater than you, and what can you do in the face of that? You either say no or, finally, you say yes. No or yes. I sensed early on what a large choice awaited me, yet I could never have known how the choice is not made once, but daily, hourly.

Outside the parlor window, I see Sister Ines. She's carrying a big basket, about to jump into the old Peugeot to speed along our gravel roads and bring food to her parents, staying a couple of days in the big guesthouse by the far fields. Day in and day out each summer, she and I used to lie on my family's little sand beach. What a luxurious life we led, swimming, eating potato chips, reading, talking about boys — we never even knew it. We groaned when we had to babysit our younger siblings.

Isabel too looks out at Sister Ines, as she starts up the car.

"Oh, there's Ali! Sister Ines." She turns to me and sighs. "I should get home."

I put my hand through the grille and she kisses it and smiles.

"Good luck, Isabel! I'll be thinking of you."

I walk outside to come around through the Enclosure gate, so I can give her a hug, as always.

I had a feeling Isabel was pregnant, when she came to visit in the middle of July, almost a year ago. I asked if she was all right, and she said yes. She was subdued, though, and I felt I should ask her more directly. "I hope you know, Isabel, you can always talk with me about anything." She nodded and thanked me, but then she changed the subject.

As Mother Heloise says, each of us lives with the choices we make. We're lucky whenever given the chance to *make* a choice, with all that life can throw our way. I pray for Isabel's continuing courage, and for Liam's too. I pray for Benny Finn, hoping he finds safe harbor.

Pentecost, June 2nd
just after Primea — 7 a.m.

I've been thinking about Pentecost — the Holy Spirit descending, in tongues of flame — as F. Julian said in Mass yesterday, did the Apostles want *that to happen? Was it a frightening feeling, or soaring? To feel changed from the inside, touched by the flames of something larger, beyond you, yet so deeply a part of you too.*

66

. . .

When I went to Italy with Ali (Sr. Ines!), four summers ago, I think I was trying to run from the idea of entering. Walking into the Basilica in Assisi, though, something called to me, once more, and more lovingly, more intensely, than ever before. I was on fire with this mystery, much as I wished I could ignore it, pretend I hadn't been, wasn't, wouldn't be again.

I'm glad to remember that moment in the Basilica. I'm trying not to doubt it.

I've been missing Isabel since she left today. I miss my family, and so many of my friends. People don't come to OLM as often as they promise to! They're busy in their own lives. Sometimes I'm so confused about what I'm doing here. Where is the tongue of flame now? Let me not lose sight of You.

Veni, Sancte Spiritus
Et emmite caelitus
Lucis tuae radium

6. Confiteor

One dream I keep having, I'm standing at the edge of a paddy. At first the paddy looks peaceful, with a few water buffalo, some old farmers bent to work. Sometimes someone else is with me, Mike or soldiers I don't know. Sometimes Liam is one of the soldiers. The dream unfolds in a few different ways, all of them bloody — the question is only, whose blood. I'll see the little girl with burning hair, or sometimes the other tiny kid, shrieking. Sometimes the dog by the well. Sometimes Sully.

I wake up sick. It can take hours to get back to sleep.

Over there, I could barely figure out who I was. Other grunts, like Mike or Sully, seemed better off, at least at first. Mike read books even in foxholes, and Sully could make a joke out of anything. Of course, later, whenever I'd visit Mike in Stamford, he'd be high from the second I walked in. He'd keep waving a lit joint in my face — *Come on, Finn, have some. This is good shit* — and he started in on heroin too.

And Sully, he wasn't around anymore to talk about it.

He was walking ahead of Mike and me along a small dirt road, and then he was on the ground, bloody, his head all twisted back, and you couldn't see one of his arms, or one whole half of him. He'd stepped on a mine. I threw up, right there in the path, calling for the medics at the same time, though he was fucking gone. The rest of us had to keep moving. There was a cleared-out village nearby and we had orders to claim hold of it. The feeling went out of my legs and my chest. It was so strange, one second to the next, how different everything was. Other people in our unit had been hit before, I'd handled it, but after Sully I couldn't feel my feet. Mike looked shaken up and sweaty. He kept wiping his face with his sleeve, again and again. I saw him touch his Saint Michael's medal.

The village hadn't been cleared out, though. Sam Hovering — the quiet kid from Long Island — got hit in the stomach and fell next to Mike. The rest of us started yelling, and falling.

It was more than that, even — it wasn't just the Cong, hiding and shooting. We realized pretty quick that there were still people in the village: women, old men, children. You can see right away, when you come into something as big and insane as that. You go around believing you've come through some crazy shit — but then you're standing in the middle of something that's on a whole other level. I couldn't hear my CO but I could see him yelling orders.

I still don't know who set fire to the houses.

. . .

69

What I want to know is, why can't the dead be forgotten? Why can't your mind become as peaceful as a graveyard? Instead, people die again and again in your memory — people you know and others you don't. They all stick with you forever, maybe even after you die. You can never be rid of them.

I glance once in a while, this summer, at the poems Mike gave me. They're very human, those poems, really. It's only on the surface they seem complicated. Stay with them enough, and you always come to something you can understand. Who was this Jesuit poet, trying and trying to put into words his passion for God and the world, and also his despair?

It's the most hopeless poems I understand best, actually. Mike dog-eared some of those pages, and I can just see him going over and over lines like *No worst, there is none. Pitched past pitch of grief … O the mind, mind has mountains; cliffs of fall / Frightful, sheer, no-man-fathomed.*

It's good, in a way, to hear a description of the worst. I mean, if you can make the effort to describe emotions like that, if you can see them more from a distance, you can feel a little more like yourself.

About a block from Isabel's apartment, the day I kissed her, I parked in front of a house with a bunch of rusting

Tonka trucks on the front walk. An old woman was shuffling along with a walker, very slow.

Isabel undid her seat belt and picked up her bag. She hugged the bag to her, one hand on the door handle. A couple of mourning doves flew to the sidewalk, pecking.

"I don't know why I told you, Benny."

I held onto the wheel with both hands. I watched the doves pecking and then flapping their wings to fly up onto an iron railing between the houses.

"It's just, I tell myself, I can't be! I *can't* be! I don't know what to do."

The old lady was slowly making her way along the block. Up on Mass Ave, a big bus groaned as it swung to a halt.

"Benny. Say something."

It felt important and necessary to hold onto the wheel, to look away as Isabel wiped her eyes with the back of her hand.

"Just say what you think."

"It doesn't matter what I think."

"It does. It does matter."

I could hear that she meant it. What really mattered, though, I knew, was to hold myself together.

"Isabel, listen, I shouldn't have touched you. And the rest of it — it's none of my business. I'm not the guy who made this baby with you. You should be asking him what *he* thinks."

"I did," she said. "Do I even need to tell you what his answer was?"

I flinched a little, but gripped the wheel. I almost couldn't stay in the conversation. I needed a wall of some kind to grow up between Isabel and me, but I also couldn't leave her alone with Liam on the other side.

She made a small coughing sound, catching a sob, holding it in, and her voice got thick with the holding. "It's like Liam can't even talk about any other solution — just go back to Yale and keep living as if this hadn't happened. And maybe he's right — I can't imagine quitting college, or having to tell my dad. But then I think Liam doesn't know what it's like, to have this — *something* — inside. This possibility."

The doves flew back to the lawn and marched to the truck on the sidewalk, and then around it, single file, as if they were on patrol.

"You can hold onto that, Isabel, if you want. The possibility."

But I realized how, whether she let this go or kept it, people would shake their heads. Everyone would have their big fat opinion.

"I'm not the only one in the picture, though. It's up to Liam too, right?"

She was waiting for me to say more, but I knew we were on the edge of something and my mind was going blank.

"Is this what happened to you, Benny? When you were in college? Did you and your girlfriend do something you weren't sure of?"

I pictured Tessa that spring, beforehand, on her bed, her black hair over the pillow, the sadness that hit her like a blast.

"We didn't talk about it, not really."

Something cold and big was floating into my chest. I would have this conversation now. I would let her ask me whatever she wanted. I saw that somehow I owed it to her, and I suddenly felt I owed it to Liam too, in a way I couldn't understand.

"Did you ever tell anyone?"

"No. Well, she had to tell her cousin. The cousin helped her find the doctor."

"And no one else ever knew?"

"*You* know, Isabel."

I pictured how I hovered outside Saint Dominic's one drizzly afternoon, afterward, trying to work up my courage to go to Confession with the new priest, the one who came when Father Connaught retired. All kinds of people went in and then came out, folding up their umbrellas when the drizzle lightened. I wasn't able to walk into the church, though. I just never did.

Tessa's most recent Christmas card had shown a picture of her baby all bundled up in a white snowsuit and with a hat of soft antlers. The card said *Peace on Earth! Love, James, Teresa, and Chloe.* Underneath, in the blank space, Tessa wrote, *Benny, I wish you all happiness. Love, T.*

Isabel and I sat a while not saying anything. It was almost peaceful. The car was like a house, and we were perched there safe inside it, watching the birds and people

73

in the heat, the dogs walking by on their leashes, sniffing the grass.

Finally Isabel asked for the key, and then she said, "I'm sorry, Benny, about everything." Then she got out and walked quickly past the little yellow trucks.

A couple days later, I had lunch with Cait on my day off. She was up from Cohasset to visit Aunt Irene and Nana, and then to check on the house. We ate cheese sandwiches in the backyard with a bag of salt and vinegar chips. Cait had brought a doughnut for each of us.

After our picnic, I lay in the shade near the honeysuckle, half listening to Cait, feeling coolness come up from the ground like the earth sighing in its sleep.

Cait had her nail polish out and was painting her toenails a peachy pink to match her fingernails. She talked about her summer waitressing job, and how she hoped to go camping up in Maine with her boyfriend, though she couldn't tell our parents who she'd be going with. It was unfair how old-fashioned they were, she said. I said maybe they just wanted to protect her.

She snorted. "I don't need protection." She waved her bare feet in the air, to dry her nails. She had little bits of tissue between her toes.

"Hey, I almost forgot. You know what Aidan just told me about Isabel?" She was walking to the kitchen stoop with her soda can and the bottle of nail polish. "He said she left Cambridge yesterday, all of a sudden."

With the screen door in hand, she paused, turning back, as if waiting for me to say something.

"Where'd she go?"

"New Hampshire. For the rest of the summer."

I felt stupidly hopeful for a second.

"Is Liam with her?"

"No, Liam's here in Milton."

"Kind of, sort of," I said. "So that's the news?"

"That's all I know. I wonder, though." She was looking me over. "Are you OK?"

I glanced at my watch, brushed away a couple ants, and jumped up, saying I had to go.

Cait hugged me on the driveway. In a low voice, like we were in on a great conspiracy together, she said, "Are you in love?"

I laughed. "Why do you say that?"

"Who is she?"

Cait's like a seagull. Spotting the tiniest thing, she'll dive for it.

I punched her lightly on her shoulder. "She's taken."

"Taken! Are you heartbroken?"

She looked so sweet and anxious, Cait standing there, her face turned up to mine.

"Yes. Yes, I am."

She eyed me closely. "Be intelligent," she said. "Don't be an idiot."

"It's not what you think."

"I don't think anything."

"Well, that's good, then. There isn't anything."

"Well, that's good."

She hugged me again, and whispered in my ear, "I'll send you a postcard from Maine. *Wish you were here!*"

It was an old family joke. Mom always used to make us write to about a hundred cousins and aunts and uncles whenever we went on vacation. We'd be hanging out in a motel somewhere, and she'd plunk down a stack of postcards on a picnic table, so we could choose from pictures of lobsters in traps, or lighthouses, or fishing boats, or impossibly white dunes against impossibly blue skies. Any postcard a Finn kid wrote, that wish would go in the last sentence, no matter what came before. *The weather's been rainy, lots of jellyfish, Eilie has the measles, Aidan broke his arm, wish you were here.*

On my way home, it occurred to me that maybe Isabel was just going to New Hampshire to have the thing done, and then she'd go back to Yale after all, to start fresh.

At an intersection in Cambridge, the light turned yellow ahead of me. I should have just waited, but I juiced the gas. I must not have been thinking too clearly. To my left suddenly there was this old silver Chevy, and a young woman inside looking at me in horror. Someone's tires screeched as I swerved, maybe mine. The woman in the Chevy must have hit her brakes or turned in the other direction. When I glanced in my rearview, she was nowhere in sight.

I pulled into a corner gas station to catch my breath. I got out for a minute and stood watching the traffic rolling by. I couldn't get the words of a prayer out of my head, the one you say sometimes after Confession: *Oh my God, I am heartily sorry for having offended you. ... I have offended you, my God, who are all good and deserving of all my love.* Cars came and went in front of me, all the same, all different, and I couldn't remember the rest of the prayer, not for anything.

Back at home, I sat out on my second-floor porch for a while, trying to calm down. One of my neighbors, an old, old Polish man, came tottering out of his house with a watering can. I watched him filling the can, walking it over to this little patch of garden where he'd planted what looked like tomatoes, lettuce, basil, zucchini, and a whole bunch of weeds. Maybe the old guy had a landlord like mine, who almost never came around to repair faucets or mow, much less help with the weeding. The old man wore a canvas hat to protect his wispy haired head from the sun.

I could feel a little of that urge to look through a lens and *find* something, catch it inside the clear space of a photo, get it so right that you could see things in it later that surprise you — light and posture and contrasts, angles, a gesture. I didn't get my camera, though. I watched the old guy bend over his garden like he was talking to it in a really gentle voice, the light hitting his white shirt and his hat.

I couldn't stop worrying about Isabel. I'd made a mistake with her that involved more than my own craziness. It wasn't some small mistake. It caught her up in something, and Liam too. The three of us were connected to this now, and any one of us could mess things up for everyone. How could I unwind that story? How had it happened? I'd have to go back to the first day I met Isabel. Or to the day in the village, or no — before that — to Tessa in my arms, some moment in her bed, that winter of college, when I was careless.

I flipped on the TV, avoiding the latest news about Cambodia and Nixon. I drank a few beers, then rolled a joint in honor of Mike Saltis and Sully and the rest of them and smoked it on my porch, listening to the sounds of families cooking dinner, kids playing together in their yards.

I still have the letter from Tessa, the one she sent me in Nam, right before the day I cracked up, where she tells me she loves me, but she doesn't think it's going to work, and she wishes me well, she'll pray for me to come home safely.

I'd been avoiding Liam, but knew I couldn't avoid him forever. So when Mom called one morning in mid-August and asked me to bring him down to Cohasset, I threw some clothes into my car and picked him up at the house.

He had some things in a bag — a new check register and some bills for Mom, Aidan's rubber boots, a couple sweaters for Eilie. On our street the trees already had flecks of yellow and red.

I wondered if somehow Liam knew about my hour with Isabel, but no, I doubted he would have sat in the car with me. On the one hand, it was just a day in August, and I was driving my brother to the shore, listening to music, like I'd done for years, and on the other, I almost couldn't see straight for the way my head was so full of the girl my brother loved.

In Hingham, where the salty smell of the water first breezed through the car, I got an irrational rush of happiness. John Lennon's "Imagine" had come on the radio, and the song felt for a minute like some great bird in the car with us, covering Liam and me with its wing.

Up ahead was the ice cream and candy store.

"Hey, Li," I said, "you want a cone?" I pulled into a space in front.

Liam shrugged. "Nah, but go wild, Benny."

Inside, I picked out all the stuff I knew Eilie and Cait loved: chocolate kisses and nonpareils, licorice sticks, jellybeans. It felt like a holiday in there, the aisles filled with mothers and babies, milkshakes whirring in the machine, kids dripping ice cream on their sandals. I felt too big for the place though, and I tried to be quick about my business, thinking how, if you had kids, you'd come buy sweet things all the time and you wouldn't feel so stupid.

Back in the car, I gobbled a handful of jellybeans and glanced at Liam. He was staring out the window, but not like he was looking at anything.

I offered him some candy.

"I haven't even had breakfast," he said.

"Who needs breakfast?"

He grunted and picked a few nonpareils from the white bag, popping them into his mouth.

"Cait told me Isabel went to New Hampshire."

"Yeah. So?"

"How come?"

Liam shrugged. "I guess she wanted to."

Some mothers with strollers were chatting on the sidewalk. I thought about just letting it go, but I wanted to be honest for once, or as honest as I could be. The Lennon song kept playing in my head.

"I know a bit about her situation, Li."

"What situation?"

"The pregnancy."

Liam was quiet for a sec. "How do you know about that?"

"She told me."

"She told you? What was she doing talking to *you* about it?"

"It just came up."

"Well, it's none of your fucking business, Benny."

A little girl, about two years old, maybe three, was leaning to lick her sister's ice cream cone. Her own ice cream plopped in a mound onto the sidewalk, and as soon as she saw it there, melting, she started to cry. Her mother, a tired-looking girl about my age, quickly threw it into the trash as the kid just stood on the sidewalk and sobbed.

A word came into my head, one my father used to use: *inconsolable. Are you inconsolable?* he'd say, and whichever one of us was the basket case would pause for a second in the midst of tears, just listening to that word. What a great rolling sound it had.

"I don't even understand," Liam said, "why Isabel told you."

"What's the difference? It's still the same situation."

"No, but since when did you and Isabel get so cozy anyway?"

"I'm sorry, all right? I don't think she meant to tell me. She was just upset."

The little girl was still crying. Now her mother was bending close, trying to coax her into licking her own ice cream. It looked like peach or something, and of course a little kid wouldn't think peach was a real ice cream flavor.

A yellow kite in the shape of a fish came into view, soaring above the stores. Someone must have been flying it near the Harbor. For some reason, another bit of that prayer, the one for Confession, rushed into my mind: *I firmly resolve with the help of Your grace.*

Liam had looked away. "So what did she say?"

"That she wasn't sure what to do."

"And that's it?" He looked at me, doubtful.

"Pretty much."

"What did you tell her?"

"What do you mean?"

"Did you give her advice? Did you tell her not to — did you tell her to have the baby?"

"Oh, right, Liam, I go around telling everyone what to do in their fucking lives. I'm doing such a fabulous job in my own."

"What did you say to her, Benny?"

"I just said she should talk to you. I said it was up to you both."

Liam pulled his fingers roughly through his hair.

"Well, it's pretty obvious that I can't have a baby in my life right now."

The kite was climbing higher, swimming on the air, swooping, then rising. A couple of kids bicycled past the store in swimming trunks, with towels around their necks, threading carefully through the crowd. The boy at the rear was scrawny, with hair like straw, the sun lighting up his freckly back.

Liam hit the dashboard with the flat of his hand and said, "Jesus Christ, Benny. What would *you* do if your girlfriend got pregnant?"

I couldn't keep the picture out — how Tessa had trembled as I'd helped her into my car after it was over. I hadn't known till then how much it mattered.

"I don't know, Li."

"Isabel has some crazy idea she can have this baby."

"Is that so crazy?"

Liam looked bewildered and furious.

"You tell me! What's not crazy about that?"

I really felt for him. "I don't know, Li. It's just, you can't have it back, once it's gone."

"I can't make decisions based on how I might feel in the future."

"How else do you make a decision, then?"

The families had scattered, some walking slowly down the street. I looked for the little girl who'd lost her ice cream, but I couldn't see her or her mom.

I couldn't think what more to say. I felt exhausted suddenly, like I'd been wrestling for a long, long time, in smothering heat, with someone invisible and dogged, not Liam only. I'd been wrestling until I was out of breath entirely.

I pulled out of the parking space and headed to our house near the water.

As Liam and I approached the small bridge over the inlet, a duck waddled out in front of us, its head glistening green-gold, its beak bright orange, followed by another one, dusky brown, and I waited for them to cross the bridge like small pedestrians. The last line of the prayer came to me out of the blue as they made a little procession a few feet from my car: *to confess my sins, to do penance and to amend my life. Amen.* In the wink of an eye, the ducks had disappeared on the other side through an opening in a bunch of bushes crammed with wild roses.

7. Sister Clare

Right as we sing Psalm 121 for Terce this morning —
June 12th — I think of Benny Finn. I love this psalm
about peace — *Fiat pax in virtute tua* — *let peace be in your
strength.* I should tell him about it.

My dream of early this morning comes to me. I was
climbing a great hill, wondering if I could reach the top. It
felt like a hill in Italy, maybe near Assisi. I had to cross
people's fields, and struggle over barbed wire. Olive trees
were on the hillside. I almost stumbled over Benny,
dressed like a soldier. He was slouched against a tree, and
I thought he was injured. "I can't go further," he said. I
tried to lift his pack, but it was too heavy. "Come on," I
said, "you can," but the words came out strangely. I could
only speak in chant. All around us it began to snow.

As we stand, singing, and face the congregation through
the iron grille in the church, I am startled to glimpse
Benny among the guests and other congregants. For a
moment I think I'm still dreaming. He must have come up
again early this morning from Somerville, before the bird-

84

song. He's in one of the last rows of chairs, looking alert and as handsome as ever.

After breakfast, I'm relieved to gain permission from Mother Heloise for a short, spur-of-the-moment parlor with him. As my formation mother, she's strict when it's called for, and she can be painfully direct, yet she has great humanity.

Mother Rita assigns Benny and me, as she often does, to the smallest parlor, which is a bit comical, given his size. He's so tall, and his legs are so long, he can barely fit into the space by the window. The New Hampshire humidity is already starting up at ten o'clock this morning, causing us both to sweat. I use my handkerchief on my face every minute or so, and hope I can jump into the shower at some point today.

I've known Benny three months already, ever since the cold March day when he helped me shovel out the old sheepfold, and we talked about the poetry of Gerard Manley Hopkins. How much of the world he seems to hold in his eyes. Their color reminds me of the burnt gold in frescoes of saints.

"I dreamed about you last night, Sister Clare," he says. "You were at the beach at Cohasset, and you had my family's old dog Lily with you."

"Oh? What kind of dog was she?"

"A collie."

I smile through the pine grille. "I love collies."

Benny shifts his long limbs in the chair.

"I have to say, I was glad to see you both — you and Lily — in the dream."

"Then what happened?"

"It was a good dream," he says. "I can't remember much of it, though. I just remember seeing you coming toward me. Lily was at your side, wagging her tail. She looked so comfortable with you, like she knew you really well. I thought, wow, how did Sister Clare find her?"

I breathe in the sea air, the faithful Lily at my side.

"So when I woke up this morning," Benny says, "I thought, what the heck? I'll go up today. My days off are Wednesdays and Thursdays right now." He studies my face, as if he's trying to decide whether to say more. "Do you think I could stay here tonight, in the men's guest-house?"

"I'll ask."

To have Benny here for the rest of the day, and tomor-row too — the idea makes me soaringly happy. This will be the first time he's stayed more than a few hours. Even if I can't meet with him again, talk with him, I will know he's here. He'll have the lunches Sister Marina and I make. I'll be able to see him through the grille in the church. I wish today's lunch could be less simple — it's just lentil soup, for the second time this week — salad, cheese, and bread. Maybe we can do something special for dessert, quick and delicious. I could ask Mother Christina Joseph if we can serve some of the strawberry ice cream we made two weeks ago.

It pops into my head, something Mother Heloise mentioned to me recently about Benny.

"I've been meaning to ask you something, for Mother Heloise."

Benny nods. I feel shy, but I take a breath and plunge forward.

"Well, you certainly don't have to do this if you don't want to. It's just, Mother Heloise is very proud of the garden you created with her, by the side of the dairy, and she wonders if you would take some pictures of it for her? She says you talked to her about photography." I don't tell Benny how insistent Mother Heloise has actually been about this. "A few pictures. She's hoping to send them to her family and friends. Her idea is to sell copies in the gift shop too, as cards."

Benny looks surprised, but I can tell he's contemplating the idea.

"You guys don't have cameras here?"

I laugh. "Yes, we have cameras. Mother Heloise just hopes that *you* will consider taking the pictures. She likes you." I wait for a moment, to see how Benny is taking this. "You know, she's an artist herself."

His eyebrows go up. What a joy, to surprise him a little. He responds so quickly, he has such openness, I think, in spite of all he's been through — a sturdy integrity, at the core.

"She's a painter." I rush on, hoping to persuade him. "I'm sure she'd love to talk to you about it. One day maybe she'll show you some of her work. Most of it is in her family's houses, but we have a few of her paintings here, inside. She studied in Italy, before she became a nun."

Benny's face radiates interest now. Ah! I think. I have caught him!

"Well," he says, "OK. For Mother Heloise. I don't know how good the pictures will come out, though."

"Oh, false modesty!"

He laughs. "Not false. I haven't even held a camera in a long time, Sister Clare. It might take me a while to get back into it."

I can see that he's already way ahead of me, though, thinking about that garden, in the light of morning and noon and afternoon, or at dusk, as the phlox shines even more boldly.

8. Wish You Were Here

I've been realizing recently, there's no way I can tell this story with total truthfulness. I mean, I can only see what's happened, really, from my own point of view. I'd have to get out of myself, see from a much greater distance, to look at the whole truth of it, and I doubt that's humanly possible.

Once in a while, though, these days, I can almost understand how Sister Clare and Isabel and Liam and I would be part of some much bigger picture, from God's point of view. I can almost imagine God catching me up by my shirttail, lifting me above my own house, and city, and country — high above the earth. I can picture — just for a golden second — how huge and complicated the world is, how impossible to count all its stories. That's a big relief — it almost gives you the benefit of jumping out of the world while still being in it — but it's humbling too, because of course you always think your own story is so central, so wildly important, and anyway you know it best.

It's been important for me, coming back to photography. With a camera, you can only take pictures of what's in front of you, right here on earth. What's visible can be transformed, though, in the process. I think I can't truly see what's in front of me sometimes until I can look through a lens.

At the end of last August, almost a year ago, I bumped into Liam in Milton. Our family was home by then, and Liam was about to head back to Yale. I helped him carry some boxes of books to Aidan's car. For a minute I thought better of it, but I went ahead and asked him how Isabel was.

He shot me a look as he tried to fit the boxes into Aidan's trunk.

"She's fine."

"Will she go back to school?"

Liam glared. "Why don't you ask her yourself, Benny? You're so close to her."

"Liam, I haven't talked to her for a month."

He hugged his arms as he looked up the street. He looked younger, maybe because he'd cut his hair pretty short, and he was barefoot.

"She's staying in New Hampshire."

"And is she still—?"

I fully expected him to bite my head off, but instead he just said, "Yeah, she is." He gave me a confused, painful look, and walked back to the house.

. . .

A few weeks later, Isabel sent me a letter. She had painted at the top an ink and watercolor picture of a red VW bug. She'd wrapped the letter around a postcard photo of a calf standing close to a cow in a field, both looking straight out, very alert. The grass was so high it almost covered the calf's bony legs. On the back the postcard said, "Dairy cows at Our Lady of the Meadow." Isabel had left the postcard blank, except for circling those words in bright blue ink. She'd written her letter in the same color.

I was grateful to her for writing, and surprised by what she wrote, its honesty. She told me Liam was more accepting about the pregnancy now, or at least more resigned, and he'd come up to New Hampshire a couple of times. She said they were talking about getting married, maybe in October.

When I first met you, she wrote, *the size of your family bowled me over: five children! I thought your mother must be a saint. And now here I am, this baby growing inside of me, and some days I'm so frightened, facing this. On good days, though, when I'm calm enough, I can breathe a little, I think I can do this. It will just be ordinary, and I can do it.*

At the end of the letter, Isabel said,

Benny, would you believe that I write to you all the time in my head? I do. I go over and over the things I might say. I'm always adding some things, cutting other things that seem old now or fruitless, searching for the right language. The truth is, I don't know how to write it all, Benny. But it's inside me, somewhere.

I could understand the part about not having the right language, only I didn't think there *was* a language that could really be right. And what did it matter, anyway? It came to me, in one breath, how I had to let Isabel go, just let her go like a kite, bouncing over the harbor and away above the ocean. It was a relief, to realize that. I felt lighter than I'd felt in a long time.

Isabel and Liam were married on a windy Saturday in October. All of us went up to New Hampshire for the family wedding, in Isabel's church, and wished them well. Isabel moved to New Haven, and they started their married life.

Two

9. Sister Clare

July 10th, 1974

10:30 a.m.

One of the cows is missing — Maud Gonne — she's pregnant — Sr. Ines is looking for her this morning with Benny and Sr. Clement.

Feast of Saint Benedict tomorrow — so much to do! I'm grabbing this moment to write here — Sr. Solange has a summer flu, so no chant lesson this morning. Ah! Freedom!

M. Heloise yesterday: "Well, Sister Clare, how might January do for your Commitment? M. Abbess and I have been thinking about Epiphany."

M. Heloise knows Epiphany is my favorite day in the calendar — the idea of the Magi making such a long journey to find a King — and discovering instead a baby in a manger. Such a humble beginning to an important life, all to be unfurled.

Splendor and sorrow, grandeur and humility, mixed in together.
So human, that divine child.

I am happy — at moments, hugely so — but frightened too. I
feel profoundly unready. M. Heloise said, "Give yourself a
chance to reflect on this, Sister Clare. You have time. You will
know if it's right. You have the support of the Community, and
my own support and love too."

＊＊Just before noon:
Benny has discovered Maud Gonne and her new calf
at the edge of the upper meadow,
hidden behind a big boulder.
Sister Ines asked Benny to name the calf, and
he named him Saltis.

10. Meadow, with Cows

This morning Mike Saltis came into one of my dreams again. In this one, he showed up at Our Lady of the Meadow, just walking across the dairy pasture on a summer day, wearing fatigues and smoking a Kool. His clothes were clean and he wasn't injured. I walked toward him, laughing. I had a thousand questions, starting with *Where in Christ's name have you been?* Something in the dream distracted me, though — a calf ran past on skittery legs, Lily herding it — and when I looked again, all I could see was Lily running around in circles on her own, across the meadow.

I only see Saltis in dreams these days. He threw himself out of the apartment window in Stamford last Christmas Eve, a couple months after Isabel's and Liam's wedding, and died in the parking lot.

I got the call from Mike's dad on Christmas Day. After Christmas Eve Mass, I'd stayed overnight in Liam's room, since Aidan was home, and Liam was up in New Hampshire with Isabel till morning.

I'd had a pretty good winter by then. I started going to the MFA on my days off, just to wander slowly through the galleries. I liked being near all that art, liked how the artists, each of them, figured out a way to devote themselves to a vision, to make it real.

I also wrote to a few colleges nearby, for application forms. They lay in the drawer with my bills, though. It was Mike who urged me to apply. The last time I saw him, in late October, he wrote up a list of schools he was sure I could get into.

The call from his dad came around four o'clock, just as the sky was losing its brightness. Mom was serving seconds on the duck, and the candles were lit. Sprigs of holly lay in the center in the silver bowl. Isabel — Isabel Finn now — looked beautiful, pregnant.

When the phone rang, I picked up in the kitchen, and as soon as Mr. Saltis said his name, I knew something was coming, sharp and clear. It was like a plane you could hear winging its way toward you, all set to drop its napalm.

Listening to Mr. Saltis, I just kept thinking what a different world I'd been in the minute Mike had done it, maybe at Midnight Mass lost in my thoughts about Isabel and Liam, or maybe driving Eilie and Cait home afterward, past the Christmas lights shining in people's trees.

The kitchen was drenched in the smell of roast duck and tangerines. On the counter was the shortbread Isabel had brought, her gift to the family. It was still unopened, wrapped in cellophane, with a red ribbon around it.

Through the haze, I listened to Mr. Saltis's voice. There would be a wake the following day, and a funeral the day after.

"Thanks for letting me know," I said. "I'll be there."

At the wake, Mr. Saltis gave me an envelope. On the outside in Mike's handwriting it said *Brendan Finn.*

The coffin was closed, with a bouquet of white roses on top, a small American flag, and a formal photo of Mike that must have been shot sometime right before his enlistment. Brown hair curled around his ears, he was smiling a mild, friendly smile, and I wondered if I ever knew him to be as self-confident, as trusting and relaxed, as he looked in that picture.

Out in the funeral home parking lot, I opened the letter. It was neatly typed, and I remembered his dad had given him a new Royal portable for his birthday the summer before.

> *Dear Benny,*
>
> *I guess by the time you read this, you'll be pissed at me. I just want to say, I can't help that, and the choice*

I've made has nothing to do with you or anyone.
Things haven't been right for me since the day Sully
bought it and we went into the village. I know you
remember. By the time I was hit myself, a few weeks
later, I was already praying to die. Losing my legs was
a lot, but it wasn't enough.

   And I know if you were here, you'd try to talk me
out of this. You have a good outlook. You've got more
trust in the world than I do. And you trust yourself.
That's big. You didn't contribute to the horror that
day, you can be glad of that. Go on and have a good
life. Finish college while you're at it. As Hopkins said,
the world is filled with the grandeur of God, and I
hope you can believe that, I hope that information is
enough for you, or you can help to make it come true.
                        Your friend,
                        Michael Saltis

On the back, Mike had written out the prayer of Saint
Brendan.

Shall I abandon, O King of mysteries, the soft comforts
of home?

Shall I turn my back on my native land, and turn my
face towards the sea?

Shall I put myself wholly at your mercy, without silver,
without a horse, without fame, without honor?

Shall I then suffer every kind of wound that the sea can inflict?

Shall I take my tiny boat across the wide sparkling ocean?

O King of the Glorious Heaven, shall I go of my own choice upon the sea?

O Christ, will You help me on the wild waves?

As I lay in the motel room bed in Stamford that night, trying to sleep, I kept thinking of that line from Mike's letter. *The world is filled with the grandeur of God, and I hope that information is enough for you.* Had Mike ever believed in the grandeur of God, though? I mean, people were still dying in Cambodia, American planes still strafing the jungles. What filled the world was war and poverty and sickness.

I kept seeing Sully in fatigues, stoned out of his mind, two fingers held up in the peace sign. Sully on his back, his head twisted, his body just destroyed and the blood rushing out to stain the dirt. Little kids in the village, the dog loping, the old people. Mike scared shitless and desperate, heading fast toward the pavement.

What would have happened if I'd thought to call Mike on Christmas Eve? I wondered if that could have made a difference. How was it possible, what my unit did? Mike would say, *For God's sake, Finn, you were in the fucking Army, you think you had a choice about any of it?* We all walked right into a new reality that day, soldiers and villagers both. And the villagers — you still don't even know them, but they stay with you forever. The old woman limping as she ran, shot down from behind. The little kid sitting by a corpse and shrieking.

The dog racing past a well, crumpling up, howling.

And always, Christ, always, here in front of me, the girl with the burning hair, who in her confusion went racing past us, when Mike threw the grenade at her feet for no reason in the world, and she flew into the air.

At the graveside the next morning it started to rain, just a light drizzle at first, then heavier. A group of us huddled under umbrellas next to the open hole, the sides of the grave covered in fake grass carpets so you didn't have to see the dirt. I held an umbrella that Isabel had left in my car that summer. It was bright blue, with a wooden duck's head for the handle. I was wearing the khaki suit I'd worn to her and Liam's wedding, and as I jammed my hands into the pockets I felt an old pack of Camels in one, a postcard in the other. I knew the card was Isabel's, the one with the photo of the cow and calf. I wrapped my fingers around it while I listened to the priest's words over Mike's grave, about Mike's love for books, and his great sacrifice in Vietnam. I was actually glad Mike wasn't there to hear some of that. Mr. Saltis read a poem he said his son liked — "Death, where is thy sting?" A few other people spoke.

Then the priest said the blessing, and it was terrible, after that, to see the coffin lowered into the earth.

While everyone said their goodbyes and then turned back to their cars in the rain, I squatted by the grave, under the blue umbrella.

"I'll look at those poems," I said. "Thanks for the prayer, Saint Brendan's. I wish to Christ you hadn't jumped. It's OK, though. And about that day — it was beyond you, Mike, it was beyond all of us."

I looked around at the graves and thought, *so this is your country now*, this small, flat area inside an iron fence. It had maybe been a meadow once, with goats or cows munching grass, but now it was all headstones and a cold, wet lawn.

A couple of old guys stood off by a truck, shovels in hand, moving from one foot to the other in the cold, chatting some. I realized they were waiting on me, so they could pitch the earth in and wrap up the job.

But I had this surprising need, all of a sudden, to give something to Mike. I felt in my pockets: my wallet, the cigarettes from the wedding, an admissions stub to the MFA. Clearly the best thing was Isabel's postcard, so I looked at it one more time — the calf on delicate legs, the cow nearby, grass covering their hooves — and then I tossed it in. It twirled down and landed right on the center of the coffin, the cows facing up.

Back in my car, I sat for a while watching the rain hurling itself at the windshield. I thought of my happy family, still in the Christmas spirit back in Milton, wrapped in new scarves and nibbling on shortbread. I couldn't shake my own devastation, though. I kind of envied Mike the decision he'd made.

We lost half the unit in ten minutes. I learned that later. I can't remember anything, though, after the girl flying into the air, hit by Mike's grenade. They had to carry me out, even though I wasn't wounded. I couldn't move, in spite of tranquilizers and orders to get up and fall in. I'd left my body and flown somewhere else, past orders or threats.

It was Mike who told me in a letter, months later, how I curled up into a ball that day, right on the ground near the well, my arms around a dead dog, my gun beside me, my uniform spattered with blood, not even sobbing.

The girl didn't fly into the air. Fuck that — she couldn't fly. She burst into bloody pieces right in front of our eyes.

I don't know how, but something came to me then, sitting there in the cemetery parking lot. It came to me like a small boat coming into harbor in the rain, right at my feet, the oars all ready. I could go to Isabel's abbey, Our Lady of the Meadow, the place where she had waited for calves to be born, the place where she'd done her thinking. If I couldn't wrap my arms around her, butt my head into her belly, kiss the inside of her sacred thigh, tell her about the

narrowness of Mike's grave and the bareness of the
graveyard, or the way the wet dirt would have covered
him completely by now, I could at least go to that place
she loved, see the cows, maybe ask the nuns to pray for
Mike's sarcastic and tormented soul. I wished I'd thought
of that before.

It took a few hours to travel up to New Hampshire in the
rain. I was pretty sure I remembered the name of the
town, but I stopped a few times to check the map. Once I'd
pulled off the highway onto the country roads, I kept having to ask directions. There were hardly any signs.

At a gas station I bought a ham sandwich and coffee.
The sandwich tasted like cellophane, but it was good to
have something in my stomach, and the coffee was hot.
The woman at the station drew me a little map in pencil,
with a small cross for Our Lady of the Meadow. I realized
I'd passed it once already.

I almost missed the place a second time, in fact. The
round wooden sign was so faded you could barely see the
letters. Pulling in, I saw a metal sculpture of a sheep starting to jump, its forelegs in the air, its back legs attached to
a large rock. I had a distant urge to take some photos of
that sculpture. It looked surprisingly light, though it must
have been heavy. I liked how that sheep was out in all
weathers, trying to make a leap.

I'm not sure what I thought the place would look like,
but I hadn't pictured it as just a few clapboard houses,

with fields and sloping orchards all around. The main building was an old restored barn. I remembered all Isabel's talk about gardens and pigs, dairy cows and beef cows, the haying in summer, but it still surprised me to see a nun go by on a tractor, decked out in a long dungaree habit, a wool cap over her white veil. A border collie trotted behind the tractor, wagging its tail. Bits of melting snow lay in spots. It must have snowed in New Hampshire.

The sky was clearing now, and I got to wondering about what I was doing up here. I almost turned around to drive home, but something kept me. It had to do with Mike. It had to do with the rain in the cemetery, and the postcard I'd buried. It had to do with Isabel in my arms in the summer heat of my car. It had to do with the island I lived on every day, how it was shrinking faster now, water lapping its edges.

I parked in a small gravel lot, near some cedars, and then I wandered around looking for the entrance, which I finally found in the main building. It was just a big door painted blue, nothing fancy. The door stood at the top of some wide stone steps, with a light over it, and the word *PAX*.

I wiped my shoes before ringing the bell, then walked into a freshly painted white foyer. On the wall hung a picture of a saint holding a shepherd's crook and a miniature church. I noticed an inner door, which came in two parts, pine slats crisscrossing over the top half. Behind the slats was a curtain.

In a minute or two, I heard footsteps on the other side, and someone pulled the curtain. A nun looked at me through the grille, curious and polite. Her habit was black, with a white wimple and black veil, and her face looked healthy and young, though I figured she could be in her fifties and it would be hard to tell. She definitely didn't look like the nuns in my parochial school. She reminded me of my Aunt Irene before her stroke, the same fine nose, the same fierce blue eyes under a sharp forehead.

She spoke some Latin I couldn't understand — and I couldn't believe she was using Latin. I just nodded like a foreigner. When she asked me in English how she could help me, I said I was up for the afternoon, and could I ask for a prayer for someone. She said she'd be glad to write down my request, and asked how I knew of Our Lady of the Meadow. When I mentioned Isabel Howell, her face softened and she looked at me more closely, saying "Ah," and Christ knows I hadn't meant to, and didn't want to, but as I stood in the presence of this dignified woman, I felt the sting at the back of my eyes, like the tide coming into an inlet in winter.

The nun introduced herself as Mother Rita and opened a drawer, bringing out a piece of paper and a pen so I could write down my request in a shaky hand. I wrote, *Michael Saltis. Died December 24, 1973.* It was hard to write that much.

Mother Rita said, "Perhaps you could write your name as well," so I added, *Friend of Brendan Finn.*

I handed her the paper, and she looked at it.

She said, "Thank you, Brendan." Then she invited me for Vespers, which would start in an hour, and to have dinner at the guesthouse if I could. I told her I had to get back to Boston. I was on shift the next morning at Children's Hospital.

"Well, you are welcome to stay as long as you can."

"Thank you, Mother."

"I'm sorry to hear of the death of your friend."

I nodded, but couldn't speak. I looked at the saint on the wall, holding his little cathedral.

"Do you know Isabel from her home in New Hampshire?"

"Boston."

"Ah."

"Her — she's married to my brother Liam. She's my sister-in-law."

"Ah!" Mother Rita nodded, smiling. "Yes! Of course. Is your name — do you have another name?"

"Benny."

"Yes! I think Isabel has spoken of you." She added, "Do you like to walk?"

"Sure. Yes, I do, Mother."

"Well, you're welcome to walk around a bit here, outside the inner Enclosure. You'll find some good paths."

She stepped gracefully back and disappeared into a hallway. I could hear the hum of conversation back there, the clatter of a pan. I could smell bread baking.

Outside I found the gift shop, which was about to close. I bought some postcards and honey, some peppermints for

Eilie and a prayer card for Mom, to add to her collection. I would have bought a book for Dad but I didn't have the cash, so I chose instead a bookmark with a picture of Saint Francis covered in birds. Some color photos were framed on the wall, for sale, one of an orchard in spring.

I put the stuff in my car and then I wandered into a stand of evergreens, and through a small orchard. I crossed the two-lane road and walked into a sloping pasture. As I started across, the sky, still changing, went from blue to violet, with a band of light yellow on the horizon against the jagged tops of trees. My shoes rustled in the wet grass. I didn't see any cows or people. What hit me was how quiet it was — no sirens, no traffic, no shouts or even laughter — only my feet, squelching in mud now, the grass brushing my khakis with water.

By the time I circled back to the abbey parking lot, it was dark. My pants and shoes were sopping, and I'd started to shiver, but I didn't feel like leaving just yet. I figured I could go to Vespers, at least. I could listen to the nuns singing.

Inside the church a few lights were on and candles were burning. There were boughs of evergreen and flowers: narcissus, jasmine, lilies. The flower fragrances mixed with pine and beeswax, and the mud on my shoes from the field. I realized that here it was still Christmas — I remembered that Epiphany would come in a few days. My family always kept our crèche on the piano till the Three Kings could journey all that way with their camels to find the Christ child in the manger. Wise Men bearing gifts. I used to love that story as a kid.

I took a seat and soon a well-dressed old man came to sit nearby, and then some other people too, and a priest with silver hair, who I figured must be the priest Isabel had mentioned once or twice, Father Julian. He wore a black cassock and thick boots. Some of the nuns must have been under the weather — their singing was sprinkled with coughs, but still the Latin song floated out like a long and colorful banner, or two banners — one on each side, alternating, like some constant conversation, calm and balanced, but full of some kind of wanting also.

A lot of the nuns looked younger than I'd thought. I wondered which was Sister Clare, and how she'd managed to choose this life of fields and chant, and whether she missed someone in her bed. *Just in her bed?* Isabel would say. How do you let go of your ordinary self, your confusion and heat and desires?

In any case, here she was, somewhere in this group — here all of them were, with their white veils and black veils, their beautiful faces I could just catch a glimpse of through the grille.

Their songs unfurled inside me and searched me out, and I didn't care then who saw my shoulders shake or the snot rolling out of my nose. I missed so many people.

11. Sister Clare

Benny's pictures of Mother Heloise's garden sweep me off
my feet. It's the stillness, the peace in them — the satur-
ated color and the precision. He added some pictures of
the dairy, and one of Father Julian, walking away from
him, down the path toward the church.

"You are a true contemplative, Benny."

He laughs. "What do you mean?"

"Each of these photographs is like a prayer."

His eyebrows go up.

"That's funny," he says. "I haven't been able to pray in
— years. I think you have to know who you're praying to,
for one thing."

"Prayer might not always look like prayer."

He's in his usual spot in the small parlor today, just
after lunch. It's the Feast of Saint James, and Sister
Marina and I had the happy chance to make scallops in
honor of the saint — a great luxury.

The photos in my lap show bee balm, daisies, daylilies,
coreopsis, phlox, true geraniums, and in the front, along
the border, lamb's ears.

"What's this one?" I point to brilliant deep-pink floating flowers, with foliage that looks a little weedy, like
ferns.

Benny bends closer to look through the pine grille.

"Yarrow."

"I remember you said there would be anemones too?"

"Yeah, they should come out in a month or so. You can
just see the leaves coming up, in that one with the phlox."

I find that picture, and see them now, the anemone
leaves filling in the lower background behind the white
phlox. My mother loves anemones.

"Did you plant all this in the spring with Mother
Heloise?"

"Mostly."

"You've made that bed look—"

"Like paradise?"

I laugh. "Yes. Like paradise."

I wave the photos in the air near the grille.

"You should become our official photographer."

Almost as if he's talking to himself, Benny says quietly,
"You love it here, don't you?"

I feel heat rising into my face. "I—"

Images come, more than words: Benny's graceful back
as he bends to pull weeds; his face at Mass, and the way he
stays seated during the Eucharist; my small cell, with the
white coverlet, the walls in need of paint; the postcards
from my parents, on vacation in the Loire river valley
right now; the frescoes in Assisi, which once fired my
heart, and which I may never see again; the neglected

state of the herb gardens; Sister Ines's beloved face across from me in choir; Isabel saying "I miss you," as she sits right with me, on the other side of the pine grille; Isabel handing baby Liffey to Liam, and the gentle look that comes then into Liam's face; Mother Heloise's hand patting mine, as she says, "Courage." I wish I could explain to Benny how complicated it all is.

"I wish I had a place like this." He looks around our small parlor, gestures toward the window at the raggedy lawn, and I laugh, thinking how poor it looks today, but I know he means the whole abbey.

"No, really," he says. "I think about this a lot. I wish I could live here."

"Well, here you are," I say.

"I mean, really live here."

"I know."

"Now what?"

Now, stay, I hear myself thinking. *Live in a house touching on abbey land. Have a dog. Dig in the garden beds, in the vegetable beds. Come talk to me as often as you can. Or — better yet — float me out of here, Benny Finn. Help me take off this habit I so love. Save me from this place I cherish, and from this effort to devote myself to something powerful, sweeping, invisible.*

"Now—" I take a breath and shrug. "Continue to be yourself."

"Myself! I have to be better than that."

"Oh, heavens, Benny, there's always room for growth. I have enormous room for growth myself, you have no idea.

It's important to be open to change."

He hesitates, and then he says, "Thank you for being here." Again he pauses, choosing his words. "I don't deserve you."

I come closer to him, put my hand on the grille. But he wags his finger at me, and says, "I know what you're going to say. It's true, though. I don't deserve you, but I'm grateful to you."

"Consider this, Benny: I am grateful to you too. I can't even tell you."

"Well then," he says. "We're a good match."

The first day I met Benny, when he helped me at the sheepfold, I could see how Isabel might have fallen in love with him: his appealing body and smile, his kindness and modesty. He was so shy and he'd been through so much. I quickly thought through the year before, and for the first time I sensed how to fill in some of the places Isabel had kept blank.

Isabel had asked a great deal of Liam, and he'd done his best, I thought, but he was so young — he had a lot ahead of him, and a lot to figure out. He was more self-confident than Benny, but he could be shaken too. Could he hold to the challenge of marriage and the coming baby? What would have to change, for Liam and Isabel to stay afloat? And what would have to happen, for Benny to be all right?

Because I could see, from the start, how much Benny was in need of something.

. . .

This summer I've been contemplating, as steadily as I can, our threefold vow of stability, obedience, and *conversatio.* It's *conversatio* I'm finding the most challenging of all, in my own life — the "remaining supple in the hands of God," as Saint Benedict says. It's impossible to be supple in each instant, though. It's something to strive toward.

Gerard Manley Hopkins knew so much about love. *My heart in hiding / stirred for a bird.* Christ is the windhover in that poem, but so is the appealing person walking through the gate or pushing a wheelbarrow up to the berry bushes. You can feel slayed, just completely ravished and broken open, on any instant in the world. And the question is — can you stay present, and stretch yourself to meet something that calls to you?

As I shoveled the dried-out old sheep manure with Benny that first day, last March, I was grateful to him for coming to Our Lady, and for shoveling beside me. I had been so hoping to meet him face to face, after all Isabel had told me about him, and here he was next to me, digging away, and laughing, and talking about all kinds of things. I loved how he listened as I recited the Hopkins poem. I was honored that he could open up to me a little about Vietnam and his friend Michael Saltis.

I confess, my selfish daydream began there, of Benny coming up to visit constantly and always, much as I tried to shame myself into letting it go.

When the bell rang for Vespers that afternoon, I walked reluctantly up to the shed with Benny, to put away the shovels and wheelbarrow. I felt painfully aware of how much I might have said to him under different circumstances, all the things on my mind, and how much he couldn't say about what mattered most to him, in love or in his memories of war.

As I shook his hand at the gate and waved goodbye, watched him walk away in his dirty jeans and t-shirt, his shoulders broad, his hair in need of a brush, I prayed for him and Isabel and Liam. I prayed for us all. And, a hopeless fool, I yearned for Benny to come again.

Am I still a fool? I gaze at this tall guy, still looking with such eagerness at me through the pine grille on this warm July day. Will he fly off and not return? So many people do. The college students who were here this summer have each gone back to their lives, and I'm not at all sure we will see any of them again. Sometimes I think about Mother Heloise, and wonder who she's loved through the years, and whether they have had the capacity to stay the course with her, to find a form of relationship that works. It's one thing to vow a life of stability, and another thing to live this vow, hour by hour, as others come and go, to know that you will be on this land, in this one postage stamp of countryside, until you breathe your last ragged breath.

. . .

July 25th, Feast of Saint James, after my parlor with B. Finn:

From Hopkins, "The Windhover":

*Brute beauty and valour and act, oh, air, pride, plume, here
Buckle! AND the fire that breaks from thee then, a billion
Times told lovelier, more dangerous, O my chevalier!*

*No wonder of it: sheer plod makes plough down sillion
Shine, and blue-bleak embers, ah my dear,
Fall, gall themselves, and gash gold-vermillion.*

12. Chant

I sent Isabel and Liam a postcard last January from the abbey gift shop, showing a photo of the dairy, up the slope from the lower field. The picture had been taken by someone in summer, and it was filled with the green of the grass, the blue of the sky.

One morning in February, I woke up to see the sun glittering on a fresh layer of snow, and it came to me how I could just go up to Our Lady again, see how it looked, all the fields covered in white. I thought maybe I could stay for a meal, help with snow shoveling. It felt odd to go north, because usually I'd gone south, to Connecticut. I wondered if it had snowed in New Haven and Stamford.

The main drive at the abbey had been plowed, but it was still a little icy, you had to go slowly not to spin out. I saw the priest striding ahead of me, the border collie eager at his side. Once I got out of my car, the peacefulness of the place hit me; it had been peaceful the first time, but in a different way. Today it was like the whole dome of sky had frozen. The buildings and fields were hushed and still, except for curls of mist coming off the roof of the church as the sun warmed it. Time had stood still too, or at least slowed down to something you could feel. I felt better, just looking at the firs against the blue sky, hearing the dog bark into the cold. I realized I felt at home here, in the snow, on this January day. It was as if this place had been waiting for me all the time.

I asked Mother Rita to give me some work, and she set me up with Sister Ines, who was scheduled to cut down a lot of young trees at the edge of a field that afternoon. First I went to the midday chant, and then I had lunch at the men's guesthouse with Father Julian. He told me about a low stone wall he'd been repairing around the bee hives, and about his time as an Army officer during World War II. He'd been involved in the landings on the coast of Italy, and it sounded brutal.

"Of course, that was a different war from yours," he said. "We understood why we were fighting. It was terrible, but at least we understood." He told me it was in Italy, after the War, that he'd met Mother Heloise and Mother Abbess. He didn't realize then how it would all unfold, how they'd come across the Atlantic to start their Foundation on this acreage in New Hampshire.

"I studied at the Abbey of Montecassino," he said, "a few years after the War. The Allies had bombed it. It was part of the German line, meant to prevent us from breaking through and going north, to Rome. The abbey had been huge and extraordinarily beautiful. It was at the top of a large hill. It was in ruins at first. But you know, it had been in ruins quite a few times in its history. Have you ever heard what its motto is?"

I shook my head, and he smiled broadly, relishing the thought of it.

"*Succisa virescit:* Having been cut down, it flourishes."

Afterward it was pretty terrific, buzzing those trees in the clear afternoon, laughing and talking with Sister Ines, laying the branches on the snow. Father Julian arrived in his boots as the edges of the sky were turning dusky and our part of the meadow fell into shadow. He brought a thermos of coffee to share, and a large chipper, which made a racket as we threw the wood in to make mulch.

I went up a few more times that winter, on my days off. I was hoping Sister Clare would show up, at the dairy or in one of the fields, or even just outside the church, but she didn't. It felt awkward, asking to meet her, so I held off. The nuns always gave me something to do on the land, and a lot of the time I got to work with Sister Ines. She was a firecracker — pure focus and energy, and I felt I could absorb some of that. She took care of the cows too, and was something else on a tractor. She told me that she and Sister Clare had grown up together, and she'd known Isabel for years.

Mother Heloise had plans for a new garden bed on one side of the dairy, and when she described in colorful detail one day how she pictured it, I had to smile. She got me to agree to help her as soon as the ground could be cultivated. She was impatient with winter.

Once, as I left, she gave me a packet of seeds for a kitchen garden — Italian basil, rosemary, and thyme.

"Do you cook?" she asked.

"Barely."

"Oh, you must learn to cook. You'll be healthier, and you'll save money too."

It was as if Isabel had introduced me to a new country, one where I could always go. And it's funny, because I started to see I could carry that inside me too. I could take it back to Somerville with me, back to the hospital. A landscape isn't just outside you. It changes how you look at things.

On one of those warm days in March that surprise you at the tail end of winter, I finally had the chance to talk with Sister Clare for the first time. I'd gotten up the courage to write to Mother Rita, asking if I could meet this friend of my sister-in-law Isabel, and she had written back after a few days to say yes, the Community had just the job for me. I would be helping Sister Clare clean out an old sheepfold.

Sister Clare welcomed me with a smile at the big gate into the Enclosure. She was wearing a turquoise bandanna over her white veil, and a bright blue down jacket.

"Benny!" she said. "Welcome! I've been hoping so much to meet you."

Walking together to the sheepfold, she and I started talking. I felt at ease with her right away, like I already knew her. She told me how important I'd been to Isabel, which surprised me a bit. She said she'd heard I was a good photographer. She said she loved to swim, and we swapped swimming stories.

Those hills of dried-out sheep shit were hard to cut into. It was warm enough that we shed our jackets. We were working up a sweat, shoveling, when Sister Clare said "Look!"

I looked up to see a hawk soaring overhead.

Wiping her forehead with a handkerchief, she said, "Do you happen to know that poem about the windhover? by Gerard Manley Hopkins?"

For a second, I felt like Mike was with us. It was a strange feeling, kind of good though. I told Sister Clare that a friend of mine had given me a book of poems by Hopkins. He'd liked that poem too.

Sister Clare stood there, looking off, like a young captain on a ship. "*'I caught this morning morning's minion, kingdom of...of—'* Oh, I knew it by heart once!"

I straightened and smiled at her, leaning on my shovel. She looked so great, in her dungaree work habit, dirty now from the shoveling, and her jaunty belt. She looked radiant. I could see why she meant so much to Isabel.

I don't know how, but I started talking then, for the first time in years, about Saltis. I explained how caught up

122

Mike had been in the War, how afterward he hadn't been able to cross back over into the regular world. He'd given most of his books away, and I should have known something was up.

Sister Clare listened, leaning on her shovel, and then she said of course when you're a soldier, you have to do things you would never do outside of war, and it must have been hard for Mike, looking back at all that, and maybe it had been hard for me too.

I couldn't answer her, not right away. I looked at the meadow sloping down to a stand of birches, white and silver in the late afternoon light. I couldn't keep Sully's destroyed body out, or the people of the village: the little kid shrieking, half-clothed, unaided. The old woman limping and stumbling right before she fell. The dog howling before someone — someone — I — put it out of its misery. The girl, a halo of fire on her head, looking for a split second as if she could fly. You know they aren't on earth anymore, but here they are, still, and here you are, holding on. I did not deserve to be alive.

"Benny," Sister Clare said, her voice coming through from someplace distant, "I'm glad you're here. And look at all we've accomplished already!"

She pointed to the barrow and clapped me lightly on the shoulder.

"Do you think we have enough for our first load?"

I nodded, wiping my face with my sleeve.

Together we heaved the barrow up the hill to the gooseberry bushes.

. . .

I wrote my first letter to Sister Clare after that March visit.

Dear Sister Clare,

    I started thinking a lot, after my conversation with you at the sheepfold, about reasons to stay in the world. I made a list in my head, and I have to say, it was a good thing to do.

    I'm still making this list, in fact, like in some letter I'm writing to God, as if God is there at all. Or who knows, maybe this is a letter God's writing to people all the time and people don't even recognize it, what do you think? Here are some items:

    meadows with cows

    sheep and sheepfolds

    dogs: Harry, Lily, and the rest

    forsythia in my neighbor's garden

    the strong coffee my mother makes

    my father's books

    It doesn't have to be something big or dramatic. It just has to be what it is. And you could say it isn't that such things are especially amazing to look at. They can be totally ordinary. It isn't beauty, only. It's something more.

    This is what I can't handle, though: I can't let myself off the hook for the awful stuff — like Sully, and my cowardly feelings when I saw him go down. I wish I could cut my mind open, and take out that part, and other parts too.

    Sincerely,

    Benny

. . .

Sister Clare wrote back to me, a letter I still have. Well, I've kept all of her letters. We've been writing each other through the spring and into this summer. This one I've been reading every few days or so lately.

Dear Benny,

I love your list of good things.

And I understand your fury at God. The terrible things — there is no easy response to these, at least I don't have one.

But consider — what if God is in the most brutal moments of a war, just as God is in one of our meadows here? What if God is utterly unrecognizable sometimes? I used to think that the sacred would be only in happiness and peace, but what if the throat filling with blood is as filled with divinity as the fish darting in a lake?

Someone told me once, God grieves for us. Could this help you, Benny, if you could believe this?

OK. I'm adding to my own list of good in the world: the owl I saw this morning before Lauds, a poem I read today, Isabel Finn, and you, my friend in sheep manure.

With love,

Sr. Clare

Dear Sr. Clare,

If I could believe God grieves for us, I could start to forgive Him. I can't think this is enough, though, is it? It's a little too much like liberal guilt. I mean, can't you just see someone wringing his hands over us, doing nothing?

    Yours truly,
    Benny

Dear Benny,

    I understand, and I have no intention of persuading you of God's presence or goodness! I have a feeling, though, that the place to start, with forgiveness, is yourself.

    Love,
    Sr. Clare

Dear Sr. Clare,

    What if I don't know how to forgive myself? What if I don't see how that's possible? I haven't told you the worst things.

    Yours,
    Benny

Dear Benny,

    How do any of us ever feel forgiven?

    Think of the world you'd like Liam and Isabel's baby to grow up in, and then be part of that world yourself.

    Love,
    Sr. Clare

In late March, Isabel gave birth to a baby boy. Mom called me in Somerville early that morning with the news. His name was Liffey Emmett Finn — the Emmett after Patrick's middle name, and the Liffey after a river in Ireland Isabel had seen on a map. I took off work and drove Mom down in rush hour traffic to Yale-New Haven Hospital. When we arrived, Isabel was alone in her half of the room. A curtain divided her from another young woman, whose children kept running in and out, chased by her husband. Liffey was bundled into a tight cocoon in the hospital bassinet. He wore a blue cotton cap with paper rabbit ears attached to the rim, I guess because it was almost Easter. Isabel said Liam had gone home to sleep, finally, and he was hoping to go to a class after that. Mom plumped up Isabel's pillows and got her some apple juice, then held and soothed the baby while Isabel went to take her first shower. Within an hour Isabel was sitting up and talking with us as she opened my present — a small blanket with fish around the rim — while the baby slept in the bassinet. I bent over him and touched his forehead.

"Do you want to hold him, Benny?"

"Sure," I said, though I wasn't sure at all — I don't usually hold babies at the hospital, and he was so small. But then, very carefully, I slipped one hand under his head, the other under his bundled up back, and lifted.

He weighed hardly anything, and holding him in my hands as he slept, looking at the small bow of his mouth, his rabbit-eared head, I felt happier than I would have thought possible. I did feel jealous of Liam, with Isabel and now this tiny boy in his life, and there was grief too, about Tessa and Mike and the others, like a shadow I tried to ignore, but something about this baby's realness, something about the way he was so stubborn and *himself* even in his sleep — even though he'd only been here for a day — less than a day — made me relieved somehow, and peaceful. The baby's fists curled tightly, like snails, and his breath reminded me of the sweet squelch of marsh mud under a tern.

"So this is my nephew."

Isabel just watched.

"You guys did a pretty good job."

"Thanks, Benny."

When Liam arrived at the hospital, after his class, you could see how proud he was of Isabel and the baby. He looked older already, and more tired than I'd ever seen him. His face softened as he bent over Liffey's bassinet.

Soon after that, I spent a day digging out some brambles on the side of the dairy at Our Lady, where Mother Heloise was devoted to reclaiming the old garden bed. "Look at this good soil," she said, "and so much sun. It would be a pity to let it lie fallow." She dug alongside me, her wiry little frame tough and excitable, until we pulled the brambles out with thick gloves and then turned over the soil and added compost to prepare for some anemones growing almost wild in another garden. Mother Heloise had big plans for this bed, I could tell by the glint in her eyes. When the first bell rang for noon prayers she straightened up, hands on her hips, and said, "How time flies! Well then, Brendan. This is an inspiring start."

13. Sister Clare

In the herb garden with Sister Clement and me this morning, as he plants the basil I've been growing from seed, Benny asks me, "What kind of a saint was she, this Saint Clare?"

Tomorrow is the Feast of the Transfiguration, and then just five more days after that will be my own Feast Day, August 11th. The weather is still hot, and in another hour the herb garden will have so much sun on it our hats won't be enough protection. Benny is sunburnt from working in the vegetable garden yesterday. He's one of our guests this whole week — a delight to many members of this Community. He says he needs time to think.

"Oh, Saint Clare was very independent," I say. "She disappointed her parents by refusing to marry."

"A rebel."

"Oh yes. She ran away from home, and founded her own order. Did you know, Benny, she became close friends with Saint Francis?"

Looking at Benny's face as he listens, the etched crows' feet by his eyes, I realize how often he is still both here and elsewhere, in the present and yet in some other spot of time as well, figuring something out.

"Sounds like she had quite a backbone," he says, placing another basil plant in a hole, sprinkling Mother Heloise's fertilizing concoction, filling the hole with soil and pressing it down, watering.

Liam has come up twice this summer, once for a parlor with Isabel and me, and once with Benny, to mow some fields. Liam and Isabel are at home in New Hampshire for the season, renting a ramshackle cottage, and I think the change of place has been healthy. Isabel's worried about going back to New Haven, though. Once Liam's in school, she thinks he'll become totally absorbed as he always does, and frustrated, having to help her care for the baby while trying to study. She's fears he'll think of her as an albatross, and that she'll never have the chance to go back to college, although I'm positive she will.

When he met me for the first time that day, Liam looked so uncomfortable, I pitied him. Somehow we got on the subject of poetry, though, and that helped. As he held the baby on his lap, he began talking about Yeats, and then we were on our way.

"I'll just go get us some water," says Sister Clement soon.

"Thank you," I say.

She looks at Benny, hand on her hip.

"How about a little nourishment?"

"I'm OK," he says.

"Well, I may have to bring something, so we don't faint," she says, and walks off, wiping her face with her bandanna.

"I've been thinking about doing something else with my life," Benny says to me, as he starts to weed around the lavender. "Something more."

"Benny, whatever you set your heart on, you'll do wonderfully," I say. The cedar mulch I'm spreading now is so fragrant, I imagine just lying down on it. I can't control my wild hope that Benny, whatever he does, will stay close by.

He smiles. "You have a good view of things."

"I see your potential."

"That's the thing — you see so clearly."

"Oh, Benny," I say, shaking my head, my hand in the mulch, but he interrupts me.

"No, you do. You must know that, Sister Clare. I have this funny image in mind, actually. You're winging your way up into the air, and just pulling all of us after you — Isabel and Liam. Me. Probably a lot of people."

I smile, although I can sense the salt tears pricking my eyes. I sit back on my heels.

"I'm glad you find something to trust in me. But what if it's you carrying people along? Have you ever thought of that?"

"I doubt I've ever done a good job carrying anyone."

He looks at the lavender, and then at me, with a directness that dives to my soul. And in this instant I realize that I have to let this dream of Benny go, inside me. I have to open all the windows and doors, and watch him fly wherever he chooses. I could love him best that way.

"I'm hoping to go into photography," he says. "I mean, to make a living at it." He waves his clippers in the air. "I know, I know — I have to go back to college first."

"That's such a good plan," I say. I am thinking to myself, *Yes, go, most definitely and with our blessing.* And at the same time I'm thinking, *Don't forget me.*

"I didn't mean to make you cry," Benny says, looking worried.

I wave my hand in front of my face.

"No, no — I'm just crying because I'm so happy for you. You're a superb photographer. It's worth all the effort it will take — college and everything. It's what I want for you. You can do it."

"Do you think so?"

"Yes. I wish you patience and determination, Benny." It's as if I see a wave of light fill his face. The wave fills him right in front of my eyes. "It will all work out beautifully, you just have to go step by step."

14. Brute Beauty and Valor and Act

I picture Sister Clare in that second, looking at me over
the herb garden, as a captain reaching down to me in the
water. *Man overboard!* someone has called, and it's me out
there flailing, or just dumbly treading. I grip her hand and
she pulls me up, as if it's effortless. And then she says,
Here. Take this. And she passes me a net, to catch fish in.
Now get to work, she says, and I do. I do.

"The Feast of the Transfiguration is tomorrow," she's
saying, as she tosses me one of her most luminous smiles,
and I bend to the work at hand.

15. Sister Clare

August 10th, 1974, just after Compline
The Eve of the Feast of Saint Clare
Pax

Today I was just straightening up from bending over the phlox, in the garden outside the parlors, when a title for a poem came to me: "Here, the Light, Inland." What will follow? How do you translate sensations and intuition into something with its own form and movement? I think I used to know how, but I'm not sure anymore. The flowers, the fragrance of the earth, my hands holding the spade, all of it wrapped into something more, and shot through with the chant's music, the light shining.

It came to me, as I stood there: could it be that this was the poem? Could it be that this was the epiphany? Could it be more than words? And if this, in this instant, was the poem, did I share in it, more than create it? Is God the poet, then? Human poets catch bits of the light.

Right then, Benny arrived to help me pull that pathetic garden into shape. It's the garden I first started with, years ago, when I was a hoverer on the threshold. He got to work on the weeds, while I planned where to put the impatiens.

So — here I am setting down the date for my First Vows. I have agreed to this with Mother Heloise and Mother Abbess:

January 6th, 1975, Epiphany

I think I can do it. I'll talk to Mother Heloise more about it tomorrow, once my family has scattered. I have five months to prepare as fully as I can. May I hold to this intention!

before Matins
1:20 a.m.
Nineteenth Sunday in Ordinary Time
Feast Day, Clare of Assisi

From "The Prayer of Saint Brendan" (one of Benny's gifts to me):

> *"Shall I take my tiny boat across the wide sparkling ocean?*
> *O King of the Glorious Heaven, shall I go of my own choice upon the sea?*
> *O Christ, will You help me on the wild waves?"*

Could I have known Benny so well, if I'd met him outside, me in ordinary clothes and on my own, not in this Enclosure? Could such trust have grown between us?

Will my life be always filled with tumult and questions? Why must I go on aching for this bond that we already share, as

I ache for a naked swim through a tangle of water lilies, or for a house full of children?

All right, then, I think. All right. Because balancing these questions and desires — so human, as Mother Heloise says — is something extraordinary, something real, each second, if only I can be present to it, if only I can be attentive and ready.

Am I right, and is it here for me? Will my patience bear any kind of fruit? I am so lonely this summer night, I confess. No grand thoughts or phrases can do away with this loneliness at the heart of the world.

I pray for Isabel and Liam. I pray for Benny. I pray for my mother and my father, my sister and brothers. I pray for all my friends. I pray for the Community and Sister Ines and Mother Heloise. I pray for good weather for the vegetables and fruits. I pray for the calves in the far field. I pray for Father Julian's health, and his restoration of the peach orchard. I pray for courage, and for understanding, for compassion and wisdom.

16. The Beauty of Ordinary Things

The sky is blue today, Sister Clare's Feast day, almost cloudless. I was up late reading the news about the impeachment proceedings, and I'm pretty tired, but as I walk up to the church for Sunday Mass I get a second wind. It's great then to hear the special prayers for Saint Clare, and to hear Sister Clare praised in the homily. Father Julian's subject is gardeners, and the nurturing of the land as a kind of prayer. A lot of Sister Clare's family and friends are here, but Isabel hasn't come up today, which surprises me. I'm relieved and disappointed, both.

After breakfast, I walk with Laude through the fields near the dairy, and I take some photos. Laude must know each inch of this land. He clearly has special spots that draw his inquisitive nose. I don't know what he'd think of poor pudgy Harry — most likely he'd see our little suburban dog as his charge, and try to herd him.

I make a cup of coffee in the men's guesthouse and read the paper some more, and then I walk up the drive for Sext and None. As I come in sight of the church, I see a young woman holding a baby. She's wearing a long skirt and a white blouse, her hair short, in curls all over her head. The baby's in a yellow sunhat and a white cotton outfit. The woman looks in my direction, her free hand shading her eyes, and then waves, and I see it's Isabel. Last I saw her was in the hospital in New Haven, the morning Liffey was born.

I give her a quick hug, and she says, "I *thought* you might be here today, for Sister Clare."

Liffey sits up in Isabel's arms, looking over his small shoulder to stare at me. His neck is sturdy. I can see a little of Liam in his forehead, but his mouth reminds me of Isabel's.

"Is Liam here?" I ask.

"No. He likes Sister Clare, but the whole thing sounds like a misery to him."

I have to laugh, looking off at the apple orchard. "The Finns," I say. "It's all Patrick's fault."

After the midday prayers, Isabel goes to the guesthouse for lunch with the family and old friends who have come up to celebrate with Sister Clare. She and Sister Clare invite me too, but I decide, I don't know why, to eat with Father Julian at the men's guesthouse. The nuns have made a pasta with summer vegetables, in honor of Saint Clare of Assisi, and they gave Sister Clare the morning off of lunch duty.

Afterward, Isabel finds me and with Liffey in her arms we walk slowly along the drive, to the beehives, and back again around the orchard. I tell her I've been helping Father Julian with the peach orchard, inside the Enclosure.

So far, the peaches are nothing much, but we hope within a year or two they'll taste better.

"Or maybe five years," I add. "Patience in all things."

As I talk, I feel in my pocket for my cigarettes, but I don't light one.

Isabel tells me how she wishes she and Liam could just stay in New Hampshire, and he could take a year off from college.

"He won't hear of it, though," she says. "He's set on forging right ahead, winning his summa cum laude, getting a Rhodes Scholarship."

"What about you?"

"What *about* me?"

"I thought you wanted to finish college too."

Isabel looks at Liffey and then at the apples glimmering in an old tree nearby.

"How can I, though? It seems impossible."

"It's not impossible."

"You sound like Liam."

"Well, Liam's pretty smart, you have to admit."

But even as I say this, I just want to fold Isabel into my arms. I can't help feeling it, and I have to be honest, I know the feeling may never leave me. That's all right, though. After a point you start to see that you can survive your own feelings, and the daydreams and nightmares that come to you. They don't have to pull you off course.

"I'm thinking of going back to school myself, you know."

Isabel looks at me with a flush of surprise, or happiness, or maybe relief.

"That's good news, Benny!"

"So try it yourself, why don't you? How hard can it be?"

There's a word my dad especially loves, and it comes to mind while I'm talking with Isabel: *sufficient.* He'll say, *Have you done a sufficient amount of research into that question?* Or, to Mom, *My lunch was sufficient today.* It's always struck me as a funny word, restrained and official somehow, but under this hot sun, with Isabel, it sounds right. Could this be sufficient, then — to see her on a summer's day, and a winter's day, to talk about our lives, to watch this little boy grow up? And to shovel sheep manure with Sister Clare, and wheel it up the hill to the gooseberries? I can have this always.

"What?" she says. "What are you smiling about?"

"Nothing."

She tucks her hair behind her ears. "I'm meeting Sister Clare in a minute. Will I see you later?"

"Sure."

"Where will you be?"

Looking at her I feel a wave of gratitude for my life. It's like Isabel and I are caught up in it, a wave and a sea beyond our imagining, bigger than us, bigger than Liam and my family, bigger than all the people I've ever known and loved, Sully and Mike, Tessa, but including them, impossible to measure. *Pace* to all the people who are beyond my help or anyone's now. *Pace* to the terrible sorrows of the world, which will never end.

Beautiful Isabel, mother of Liffey, wife of Liam Finn, friend of Sister Clare, sister-in-law to Aidan and Cait and Eilie and Brendan. How many forms love can take, after all.

I look at the cedars and the orchard, and into Isabel's blue-green eyes.

"Benny? Where will you be?"

"I'll be here, Isabel Finn."

She looks at me carefully, a new fine line etched lightly on her forehead, and then she gives me one of her best smiles.

"Well, I'll see you here then, Benny Finn."

She turns and walks along the drive, my nephew contemplating me soberly, his head in the yellow sunhat bouncing over her shoulder.

As I watch them go, it hits me how courage comes from some wild source in the world — something divine, *grace* — and I don't know how, I don't know how, but when you have love, in whatever form it comes, you should just say yes to it, and keep saying yes, until you say your last word and breathe your last breath entirely.

You're here, then, I know. Maybe I've been writing to you all my life, thinking I was writing to someone else, someone loved, or just talking to myself, in between waking and sleeping, where I can only be honest, just totally open, because a person is a window, really, a window you can see straight through. I can't figure out why it's taken me so long to understand this. I used to think of myself as an island other people couldn't get to except sometimes by boat, and even then it would depend on the weather and my own willingness to show myself. But I understand now. I could be across an ocean, boat or no boat, I could be in another country. Invisible, you were always here.